Magic Beans

www.**davidficklingbooks**.co.uk

MAGIC BEANS
A DAVID FICKLING BOOK 978 0 857 56043 8

Published in Great Britain by David Fickling Books,
a division of Random House Children's Books
A Random House Group Company

This edition published 2011

1 3 5 7 9 10 8 6 4 2

The Random House Group Limited supports The Forest Stewardship Council (FSC®),
the leading international forest certification organization. Our books carrying the FSC label
are printed on FSC® certified paper. FSC is the only forest certification scheme endorsed by
the leading environmental organizations, including Greenpeace. Our paper procurement
policy can be found at www.randomhouse.co.uk/environment

Set in Sabon

DAVID FICKLING BOOKS
31 Beaumont Street, Oxford, OX1 2NP

www.kidsatrandomhouse.co.uk
www.totallyrandombooks.co.uk
www.randomhouse.co.uk

Addresses for companies within The Random House Group Limited can be found at:
www.randomhouse.co.uk/offices.htm

THE RANDOM HOUSE GROUP Limited Reg. No. 954009

A CIP catalogue record for this book is available from the British Library.

Printed and bound in Great Britain by Clays Ltd., St Ives plc.

Magic Beans

A Handful of Fairy Tales
From the Storybag

David Fickling Books

☆ Contents ☆

☆

The Six Swan Brothers

Retold by Adèle Geras

Illustrated by Ian Beck

There was once a King who had seven children: six strong sons and a daughter whose name was Cora. They lived in a palace on the shores of a lake, and they loved one another greatly. Their mother died on the very day her daughter was born, and the King and his sons mourned her for a long time. Later, when Cora grew up, laughter returned to the palace, and the days were as like one another as beads on a string, all sparkling with happiness.

Then one day, the King went hunting in the forest. His men rode with him, of course, but he soon left them far, far behind him. He had caught sight of a wild boar, and plunged after it into the places where the trees grew closest together, and branches knotted into one another overhead to make a canopy that kept out the light of the sun.

All at once he came to a clearing, and there was no sign of the boar. He realized that he was lost and called to his men, but there was no answer. Suddenly a woman stepped out from between the dark columns of the trees. The King knew at once that she was a witch, because her head nodded and nodded, and her yellow eyes were

weak and rimmed with scarlet.

'Greetings, good lady,' he said in as firm a voice
as he could manage. 'Will you show me the best
way home? I fear I am lost.'

'I have the power to send you home along
straight paths,' the woman whispered, and her
voice was like a rusty blade. 'But you must do
something for me in return, or I will leave you
here alone and soon you will be nothing but a
complicated arrangement of bones.'

'I will do anything,' said the King, for there
was nothing else that he could say.

He followed the Witch to her hut, and there
beside the fire sat a beautiful young woman.

'This is my daughter.' The Witch twisted her
mouth into something like a smile. 'You will
marry her and make her Queen. That is my
condition.'

'It will be my pleasure,' said the King, and
he took the young woman's hand and set her on

his horse. The touch of her fingers filled him with a loathing and disgust he did not understand. She is beautiful, he told himself as they rode together. I should be happy, but her eyes are full of ice and darkness and her red lips seem stained with poison. He made up his mind that she should never know anything about his children, for he was sure that she would harm them if she could. And so, he took the Witch's Daughter to a house near the palace, and said to her:

'You will stay here only until I make all ready for our wedding, my dear. Everything must be perfect.'

And she was satisfied.

That very night, the King took his children to another castle, which was so well hidden in the green heart of the forest that even he could not find it without help. He had in his possession a ball of enchanted yarn, which a wise woman had given him, and if he threw that along the ground a little way, it unrolled all by itself, and showed him the path he had to follow.

So there they stayed, the King's six sons and Cora, his little daughter, hidden and safe, while the King and the new Queen celebrated their marriage. After the wedding, the new Queen noticed that he was away from the palace almost every day, and she became suspicious.

'He is hiding something from me,' she said to herself, 'and I will discover what it is no matter what I have to do.'

She summoned the stable-hands, and said to them: 'My husband leaves my side each day, and goes somewhere. Tell me,' she whispered, and her

voice was like treacle. 'Tell me where he goes, and I will pay you in gold pieces . . . more gold pieces than you will ever count.'

And because gold has the power to bend and twist even the strongest will, the stable-hands told her of the magical yarn, and of what it could do. Then, one day when the King was visiting a neighbouring country, the Witch's Daughter crept to the Treasury. There she found what she was looking for, and she took it and put it into her pocket.

She followed the silver thread as it unwound between the trees, and at last she came to the castle where the King's children were hidden. She arrived at dusk and saw six handsome young men returning from the hunt.

'Those are my husband's sons,' she said to herself. 'I am certain of it.'

When she considered how much he must love them, a bright flame of hatred leaped up in her

heart. 'It is fortunate,' she thought, 'that my husband is far away, for I have work to do.'

She looked no further, and so she never found Cora, who was in her chamber, high up in the tower. The magic thread led her back to the palace and rolled itself up behind her as she walked.

The Witch's Daughter locked herself up in a small room and cut out six shirts from white silk. Then she began to sew with a long and wicked needle that caught the light as she worked. She sang a spell as she sat there and she sang it six times, once for each garment:

'White as Ice
silken stitches
gifts I bring.
Hearts may yearn
but flesh will know
how feathers grow
from poisoned silk
smooth as milk.
Turn and burn
turn and burn
turn limb to wing.'

When the garments were ready, the Witch's Daughter unlocked her door and went to find the ball of enchanted thread. At the edge of the forest, she spoke these words:

'Your master returns tomorrow, but for now you are mine. Find them again, for the last time.'

The silver thread slipped away between the trees, and the Witch's Daughter came to the hidden

castle once again. Cora saw her from the high window of her chamber, and immediately she knew that something terrible was going to happen. She hid behind the curtain and peeped out at the stable yard, where her brothers were gathered, back from the day's hunting.

'Welcome, madam,' said the eldest. 'Our house and hospitality await you, as they do every stranger lost in the forest.'

'I am not lost,' said the Witch's Daughter. 'I have brought you gifts from the King, your father. See, here is a shirt for each of you, made from white silk.'

The young men took the shirts, and before their sister could cry out to warn them, they had thrust their arms into the sleeves.

'You will see,' said the Witch's Daughter. 'They will become like second skins.' She turned and was gone, swallowed up in the darkness between one tree and another.

Cora found she could not move. She went on staring down from the window, thinking that perhaps she was mistaken, and perhaps her heart should not be filled with dread and foreboding. But her brothers' beautiful necks were stretching and stretching and their heads shrinking and shrinking and their brown arms flapping and growing white and soon there was nothing left of men in any of them, and the air was filled with the sound of beating wings, as six swans rose and moved along the soft currents of the evening breeze towards the sunset beyond the forest.

'Wait!' Cora called after them. 'Wait for me!' But they had disappeared and she was left alone.

After they had gone, she was cold with fear and the sound of her own breathing was as loud in her ears as a sighing wind. She did not know whether to try and make her way to her father's palace, or to stay where she was and hope that he would find her. In the end, she decided to leave the castle, for the rooms were full of silence, and frightened her. Cora longed to weep for her poor brothers, but she knew that she had to follow them at once, or they would be lost for ever. She filled a basket with bread and hard cheese and took her warmest cloak to cover her, and set out for the forest.

Cora walked and walked through the night and through the following day, between bramble bushes thick with thorns like little claws, and over twisted tree roots buried in the earth; with no moon to guide her and the calling of night birds to chill her blood. She put one foot in front of another all through the black hours and at last

13

the dawn came. The young girl looked around her and recognized nothing, so she went on, searching the sky for swans, listening for the music of their moving wings and still, always, putting one foot in front of another. As night was falling, she came upon a hut. Her legs were stiff with weariness and her feet hurt from walking.

'I will see,' Cora said to herself, 'whether perhaps some kind woodcutter will let me rest here for a few hours.'

She knocked at the door of the hut, but it stood wide open. Whoever had once lived there had long ago moved on. She sank on to a bed in the corner and slept.

And as she slept, she dreamed. In her dream, six swans flew in through the window and stood around the bed.

Cora cried out: 'Why are you not the brothers that I love? Where, where are they?'

'We are here,' said a voice, and Cora thought the voice was speaking in her head, and opened her eyes at once, for surely that was her dear brother speaking? It was then that she saw them all, standing around her in their glorious human shape, gazing down and smiling.

'There is no time for joy,' said one. 'We are allowed to return to our human forms for a few minutes only, every evening, and after that we are swans again.'

'Is there nothing I can do?' Cora wept. 'I would do anything . . . anything in the world to break the spell.'

'What you would have to do,' said her youngest brother, 'is too much.'

'Nothing is too much,' she said. 'Tell me.'

'You must weave six shirts from starwort and river reeds,' he said. 'One for each of us.'

'I will do it,' Cora said. 'I will walk beside the rivers and the lakes and I will do it. It will take time, but in the end you will be men again.

'But,' said her eldest brother, 'you must not speak a single word nor make a single sound until the starwort shirts are on our backs, or the spell will never be broken in this lifetime.'

'Not a sound?' Cora felt her heart like a knot of hard wood in her breast.

'Not the smallest sound in the world,' he answered, 'or we will be swans for ever.'

'It will be hard,' she said, 'but I can do it.'

They nodded and went to the door of the hut. The sun's last rays slanted in through the window and then there was a storm of snowy feathers and Cora saw the swans rising into the mauve twilight and growing smaller and smaller as

their wide wings bore them away.

She started her work the very next day, and for many weeks all she did was wander beside rivers and streams and little brooks, picking starwort and the stoutest reeds that she could find, preparing herself for the weaving she would have to do. She took shelter under trees and in caves and hollows, and the rain fell on her and the sun burned her, and all the words she was forbidden to speak buzzed in her head and fixed themselves into rhymes which she said over silently to herself without the smallest breath of sound passing her lips. This is the song that Cora sang in her heart as she worked:

'*River reed and starwort stem*
cut and dry and weave and hem
twist and stitch and pull and bind
let white silence fill my mind
gather plant and gather stalk
stifle laughter stifle talk
sew and fold by candlelight
all the hours of every night
like a statue let me be
till my brothers are set free
freeze my words before they're spoken
let the evil spell be broken
river reed and starwort stem
cut and dry and weave and hem.'

The weeks passed and the months and the making was slow and hard. At first, Cora's fingers bled from working the sharp grasses but, after a while, she grew used to the weaving and at the end of the year, when the snow began to

fall, she had finished one shirt, and she folded it
carefully and put it into her basket.

One day, when Cora was sitting in the
lowest branches of a tree, a Prince came riding
by on a fine white horse, and his courtiers came
with him.

'Look, Your Highness,' one said. 'There's a
young woman in this tree. Shall we pull her
down?'

'Leave her,' the Prince said. 'I will speak to her
and ask her kindly to step down.'

Cora did step down when he spoke to her, but
not one single word did she utter in answer to
his questions.

'She cannot speak,' the Prince said to his men.

'She is mute.'

To Cora he said: 'I will take you back to my castle and you shall be dressed in the finest gowns and I will hang necklaces of silver round your white throat, for you are the bride I have been seeking.'

And so she went with him. She married him and lived in a castle and her days were easier. Still, she did not make a sound, and still she had to wander the country round about, searching for river reeds and starwort stems.

By day, Cora worked at her loom, and by night she slept in a soft bed next to the husband she had grown to love. She would have been happy, but for the Old Queen, her mother-in-law. Always, she felt her presence, as if she were a black spider hanging in its web in a shadowy corner of the room. The Old Queen's hatred touched Cora like a breath of cold air. She spoke openly to the Prince, saying: 'You are a fool, my son.

Cora is no mute, but an evil enchantress. See how her eyes widen! She knows I can smell secrets all over her. Oh, she is not what she appears!'

'Hush, Mother,' the Prince would answer. 'One more wicked word and I will banish you for ever.'

The Old Queen smiled, and soon her dark words were for Cora's ears only, and she was careful, very careful, to say nothing when her son was nearby.

The months passed. Cora continued to weave, and soon two shirts were finished. She put them into a cedar-wood chest, folding them carefully so that the prickly stems did not break, and then she set to work on the next garment. And after a time, her first child was born. During the birth,

she could not cry out when the pains gripped her, but she was glad to be suffering, for soon, she knew, her own baby would be there, nestled close to her breast.

As soon as the child was born, the Old Queen appeared at the side of the bed. She picked up the baby.

'I will wash him,' she said to Cora, 'and return him to you.'

So Cora slept, and when she woke, her arms were empty. She looked into the cradle and that was empty, too. The Prince and his mother stood by the bed, and the Prince was weeping bitterly.

'She has devoured her own baby!' the Old Queen shrieked. 'Look at her mouth! Her mouth is full of blood! Throw her to the wolves in the forest!'

Cora shook her head from side to side, and threw herself from the bed, and clung to the Prince's knees, but she did not speak.

'No,' said the Prince, and he lifted her up. 'I will not believe that you have done such a thing. I know you are innocent. And you, Mother, will never speak such poisoned words ever again, on pain of banishment.'

Cora wept and wept. She wandered through the long corridors of the castle like a madwoman, peering behind every curtain, and listening for the faintest sound of a crying child. The Old Queen watched her. She was the one who had smeared Cora's mouth with lamb's blood. She had stolen the baby and sent it far away to be cared for by one of her own maids in a cottage beyond the mountain, but no one in the palace knew this secret.

Two years went by. Cora continued to weave the stiff stems of the starwort plants into a garment, and there were three finished shirts folded into the cedar-wood chest in her bedchamber. Then, in the spring of her third year of marriage, she was once more expecting the birth of a baby. Cora felt the Old Queen watching her as she grew large; felt an icy wickedness reaching out to her, wherever she went.

When Cora's second child was born, the Old Queen stayed far away, and instead allowed the servants to attend her daughter-in-law. One of them came to her after the child was born, and gave her a glass of cool water to drink, but this woman was the Old Queen's creature, and did her bidding at all times. She had put a sleeping draught into the cup and before long, Cora's eyes closed and she slept.

When she woke up, the baby had disappeared, and the blood was caked and dry in the corners

of her mouth. Once again, the Old Queen shrieked terrible accusations at her son, and once again his wife lay silent and turned her face to the wall. The weeping Prince stood at the foot of the bed and refused to believe his mother. And Cora once again became like a madwoman, fretting and weeping and roaming the dark corridors in absolute silence.

After five years, five shirts were ready, and lay carefully folded in the cedar-wood chest. Cora began to dream of the day when the spell that bound her brothers would be broken for ever. Then she found that she was pregnant again and her heart was full of fear. Still, she did not stop weaving the dry stems of river reeds and the

green starwort stalks, either by day or by night.

On the day that her third child was born, the sixth shirt was complete but for the left sleeve. When my baby is here, Cora told herself, I will finish it and all will be well for ever.

When the baby was born, everything that happened twice before, happened again. This time, the Prince had to believe his mother and he condemned Cora to death. She would be burned at the stake, he told her, weeping, because that was the customary punishment for witches.

As the time for the execution drew near, Cora went to the cedar-wood chest in her bedchamber and unfolded the starwort shirts that she had made. She carried them as she went to the stake,

and all who saw her wondered at the strange garments that filled her arms as she walked. Cora thought of nothing but her brothers, and she closed her eyes and prayed for a miracle.

Then, all at once the air was filled with the sound of beating wings, and the crowd looked up and saw six white swans flying overhead. Down and down they fluttered to where Cora was standing, and they surrounded her in a cloud of feathers. Cora took a shirt and covered the first swan, and as she did so, the bird's neck shrank and shrank, and its head grew and grew and soon a man stood before her. She did the same with the other shirts she had woven, and there all at once were her six beloved brothers: complete men but for the youngest who, because she had not woven the left sleeve of the sixth shirt, still had one swan wing. Cora cried out with joy and her brothers kissed her and held her in their arms and rejoiced in their new human forms.

'You have saved us, little sister,' they said. 'You have saved us with your silence, and now your own life is in danger. Speak. Tell your husband everything.'

Cora said: 'My heart is singing to see you again, my brothers, and you, my dear husband, must now know the truth, which I could not speak before.'

She turned to the Old Queen and pointed at her. 'You took my children from me and murdered them. You are the wickedest of women.'

'No, no,' cried the Old Queen. 'How could I murder my own grandchildren? They are living in a cottage beyond the forest.'

The Prince spoke sadly: 'You may not have murdered them, Mother, but you were willing to stand by and see my wife go to her death. You will perish instead of her.'

And so the Old Queen was burned at the stake, and Cora's children were brought back to the

palace and lived happily there for many years, listening over and over again to the story of the six swans. They knew that it was true, because the youngest of their uncles still had one wide, white wing hidden under his cloak.

The Twelve Dancing Princesses

Retold by Anne Fine

Illustrated by Debi Gliori

Once upon a time, in a faraway place, there lived a king who had twelve daughters. Some were pretty, and some were clever, and the youngest was as rosy as the dawn.

But was the king pleased with them? No, he was not. For each morning, as the sun rose, his daughters' nurse tapped on his chamber door and showed him a pile of tattered shoes.

'Again, Nursie?'

'Again, Sire.'

And the two of them stared forlornly at the twenty-four tattered shoes and shook their heads in amazement. For no one in the palace could understand how twelve girls could wear their freshly-stitched shoes to ribbons in a single night.

Each morning, as the sun crept over the palace wall, the king sent for his grand vizier.

'Again, Sire?'

'Again, Grand Vizier.'

And the king sighed. And the nurse sighed. And the grand vizier sighed. And all of them wished that the queen was still living, so that she could speak sharply to her daughters.

After his morning coffee, the king sent for Letitia. And Lottie. And Lola. And Lulu. And Louisa. And Lily. And Libby. And Lavinia. And Lena. And Laura. And Lisa. And Lara.

In they skipped. 'Morning, Papa!' 'Morning, Papa!' 'Morning, Papa!' 'Morning, Pa—'

But he was in no mood to listen to their chirruping.

'Daughters!' he interrupted, pointing sternly to the heap of ruined shoes. 'Have you been dancing?'

And the pretty ones giggled, and the clever ones were silent, and the youngest one peeped at her bare toes.

'Now, girls,' scolded Nursie. 'Tell your father how it is that I can shoo you into your high, high tower room, and sit outside all night and not hear a peep, and in the morning all your freshly-stitched shoes are danced to ribbons.'

'Again!' scolded the grand vizier.

And still the pretty ones giggled, and the clever ones said nothing, and the youngest one peeped at her toes.

So the king sent them off with Nursie as usual, in disgrace. Then he spoke to the grand vizier.

'Easy enough to trick poor old Nursie, with her

thin grey hair and her clouding eyes. Let them try tricking *you*!'

So the next night it was the grand vizier who shooed the twelve merry princesses into their high, high tower room, and sat outside the door and heard nothing.

And in the morning, all the freshly-stitched shoes were danced to ribbons.

'Right!' stormed the king. 'Easy enough to fool the grand vizier with his beard down to his knees and his head full of worries. Let them try tricking *me*!'

So the next night it was the king himself who shooed his daughters, twittering like sparrows, into their high, high tower room, and sat outside all night.

And in the morning, all the freshly-stitched shoes were danced to ribbons, as usual.

Then the king lost his temper. Calling the grand vizier to his chamber, he made a proclamation and ordered him to write it down.

> *I, the king, proclaim that*
> *Whosoever shall solve the mystery*
> *of the twelve dancing princesses*
> *(viz: where they go,*
> *what they do,*
> *and how their shoes are*
> *danced to ribbons)*
> *shall choose his favourite for a wife,*
> *and have my kingdom, too,*
> *when I retire or die.*

Nursie was horrified. 'But this Whosoever will see my precious girls in their nightgowns,' she wailed. 'And that won't do at all.'

'It will be perfectly fitting,' the grand vizier assured her. 'Because this Whosoever will soon be the husband of one, and the brother-in-law of all the others. So he won't tell.'

'But what if he *fails*?' wept Nursie. 'Then this Whosoever might travel far and wide through our dominions telling of my girls in their nightgowns.'

But the king had had too little sleep to be reasonable. Snatching the quill from the grand vizier, he scribbled at the bottom of the proclamation:

> *And Whosoever fails shall*
> *lose his head.*

'Happy?' snapped the king.

All the blood drained from Nursie's face. The grand vizier trembled. But before he could summon a word of wisdom or warning, the king

had given the order to send the proclamation far and wide.

And far and wide the word spread. A kingdom! And a princess! Simply for staying up all night and keeping your wits about you! Young men came running: princes and paupers; butchers and candlestick makers; huntsmen and stable boys; beggars and woodcutters; minstrels and bird-catchers – everyone you could think of (except for the shoemakers, who were already doing very well). Soon there were so many waiting outside the palace walls that the grand vizier could only give them three nights each. So every evening the staircase of the high, high tower rang with some man's confident footsteps as he ran up to

sit outside the princesses' door. And on his third and last morning, the staircase was deathly quiet as, sadly, he struggled again.

And through the taverns and market-places of a dozen kingdoms, the same tale was told. 'I heard it all went well. Paul (or Peter, or Percival, or Pedro) spread his cloak outside the door of the princesses' high, high tower room. And Letitia (or Lottie, or Lola, or Lulu) came in her night-gown and handed him a goblet of the finest ruby wine. "Good night," she said prettily enough, and shut the door. And though Paul (or Peter, or Percival, or Pedro) heard nothing, by morning, all twenty-four shoes had been danced to ribbons!'

Years passed. Till one night a soldier who had fought his share of wars and was no longer young, saw something flapping from a tree in a dark wood.

It was the proclamation, torn and faded. The soldier read it through.

'Well,' he said. 'The hand of a princess is a fine thing to win. And I could bear with a kingdom, so long as I had a grand vizier to run it for me.'

He read down to the last line.

> *And Whosoever fails shall*
> *lose his head.*

'Well,' said the old soldier. 'I have lost two of my fingers and all of my youth in the king's wars. But not my courage. Losing your head is a high price to pay for failing. But I think I shall put myself to the test.'

And on he walked through the dark wood, till

he caught up with an old woman dressed in black, hobbling along the path with a basket.

'Give that to me, Old Lady,' said the soldier. 'For even if it's filled with rocks, it will be lighter than any pack I carried in the wars.'

'Wars!' grumbled the old woman. 'Crops trampled! Cottages burned to ashes!' But she handed him the basket gratefully, and to be pleasant in return, asked him where he was going.

'Laugh if you will,' said the soldier. 'But I hope to discover the secret of the twelve dancing princesses, and win a wife and a kingdom.'

The old woman looked him up and down, scars and all, and told him: 'I should think you would make a sensible enough king. And though I should not like to marry you if I were rosy as the dawn, for the eldest princess you will be a fine match.'

Then, when they parted, she gave two things to the soldier.

First, a shabby black cloak. 'It is a lot more precious than it looks,' she warned. 'When you put it round your shoulders, you will become invisible.'

Then, some advice. 'It is a lot more important than it sounds,' she warned. 'Don't drink the wine the princess brings to you.'

So the soldier went on to the palace and told the king and the grand vizier that he wanted to try his luck. The grand vizier looked at him sadly, because it seemed to him a shame that a man should lose two fingers (not to mention his youth) in the king's wars, and then come to lose his head, too. But the rule was that anyone might try. So as the sun sank behind the palace walls,

the soldier climbed cheerfully up the steps of the high tower, and spread his shabby black cloak on the stone floor outside the princesses' door.

Out came the eldest (in her nightgown) to offer him a goblet of the finest ruby wine. But, remembering what the old woman in the dark wood had said, the soldier turned away towards the tower window and talked admiringly of the king's dominions as he poured the wine secretly into his beard, and down his thick fleecy jerkin, and into the plant pot at his side.

'Such lands!' he cried. 'Such forests and mountains and rivers and cities!'

'Yes,' said the eldest tartly. 'And don't be too confident that they'll be yours.'

And she shut the door firmly in his face and went back to her sisters.

The soldier stroked his grizzled beard. Well, he thought. The old woman was right. *She'll* be a match for a soldier.

Then he lay down and very quickly began to snore, as loudly as he could.

As soon as they heard him, the twelve princesses leaped out of their beds and threw off their night-gowns and opened all their chests and boxes and drawers, and lifted out their fine robes and jewels and coronets. Giggling and chattering, they helped one another into their gowns and silk stockings and freshly-stitched shoes, and each took a turn admiring herself in the looking-glass whilst the others tripped lightly around the tower room, practising their spins and twirls and pirouettes.

But the youngest kept looking anxiously at the door.

'Something's not right,' she fretted. 'I feel uneasy, as if this is the night we'll be discovered.'

'Silly!' scoffed the eldest, taking her hand and tugging her towards the door to peep at the snoring soldier. 'How many young men have we fooled already? Too many to count. Why should this Grizzlebeard cause us any trouble? You can hear how deeply he's sleeping already. Even without the wine, this soldier would have lost his head!'

And the soldier snored on, and shifted slightly on the shabby black cloak so that his foot went hard up against the heavy oak door, keeping it open a hair's breadth when they let go. Through the crack, he heard the footsteps turn from merry and prancing to stealthy and creeping as the eldest daughter clapped her hands and, as if by magic, her bed sank into the floor and a trapdoor opened.

Hastily, the soldier jumped to his feet and

swung the shabby black cloak around his
shoulders. Silent as moonlight, he pushed open
the door, and was just in time to follow the
youngest as she stepped on to a secret staircase
hidden in the floor, and followed her sisters
down, down, down inside the palace walls.

Down past where the king was sleeping in his
chamber.

Down past where the grand vizier stroked his
beard and worried about high affairs of state.

Down past the kitchens and wine cellars.

Down under the earth, where the staircase was
so dark that the soldier mistook his footsteps and
trod on the gown of the youngest.

'Sisters!' she cried. 'Something's not right!

Someone has stepped on my gown.'

'Silly!' 'Silly!' 'Silly!' 'Silly!' The message passed like an echo from the eldest, through the middle sisters, back to the youngest. 'I expect you have just snagged your hem on some rusty old nail in the wall.'

And none of them stopped to listen or look. So soon they stepped out at the bottom of the stair-case, and the soldier found himself dazzled, for they were in a gleaming grove of silver trees.

'Can this be *real*?' he whispered to himself. 'Silver trees under the earth? Or did I forget the old woman's good advice, and drink the wine?'

And, to be certain, he reached up to take a twig from the nearest tree.

Crack!

The youngest sister's hand flew to her mouth. 'What was that? Oh, sisters! Did you hear?'

And the message came back from the eldest, like an echo, eleven times over. 'You goose!' 'You

goose!' 'You goose!' 'It's just one of our princes, clapping for joy as he hears us approaching.'

And none of them stopped to listen or look. So the soldier hurried after them, into a second grove that gleamed even more brightly than the first because the trees were all of gold.

'Gold leaves!' breathed the soldier in wonder. 'Who would believe it?' And to prove that it was true, and he had seen it, he snapped off a branch.

Crack!

The youngest sister trembled. 'Sisters! Surely you heard that! Something is very wrong!'

And the message came back like an echo. 'You dilly!' 'You dilly!' 'You dilly!' 'It is only one of our princes dropping his oars in the rowlocks

of his boat as we approach.'

And nobody stopped. So the soldier followed them as far as a grove so bright and glittering it hurt his eyes.

'Trees of diamonds! Trees of diamonds under the earth! Sparkling brighter than frost. Glittering more brilliantly than sun on water.'

The soldier's hand crept up, unbidden, and—

Crack!

A third branch was in his hand.

The youngest tore at her hair in fright. 'Now, sisters, I am sure there is something wrong, and we shall be discovered!'

'You ninny!' 'You ninny!' 'You ninny!' The mesage

came down the merry line from the front to the back. 'That crack you heard was just the first of the fireworks our princes are sending up to greet us.'

And no one stopped. So the soldier kept after them, down to a still lake where twelve little boats with twelve fine princes in them rocked on the water, waiting.

Each princess in turn stepped in with one of the princes. The soldier, thinking the boats looked more pretty than strong, thought it safest to share with the youngest. So, keeping his shabby black cloak wrapped firmly around him, he stepped in behind her, and sat as still as stone.

And almost as heavy, it seemed. For before they were even halfway across, her young prince was grumbling. 'This is a weird and wonderful thing. I'm sure I'm rowing as hard as ever I have before, yet our boat falls further and further behind the others.'

The youngest princess bit her lip, and thought it was all very well to be called ninny and goose and dilly by your sisters. But a prince is different. So, though she was still uneasy, all she dared say was, 'Perhaps the night's warmer than usual,' and, 'Perhaps you're more tired than you think.'

Soon, though, even their slow boat reached the far side of the lake, where a glorious palace, far finer than their father's, stood proudly on the shore. Its walls of pearl glowed in the moonlight, and its battlements of ivory gleamed under the stars. The most magical music poured from its casement windows. And there were so many glittering guests that they spilled, laughing, out of the several ballrooms on to the

terraces and into the gardens.

And how they were dancing! Every last one of them! Round and round, up and down, to and fro, here and about. As the trumpets swelled and the horns echoed, the palace and gardens rang with their laughter. First, the soldier watched from the safety of his shabby black cloak. Then the music and merriment made him bolder, and he joined in, leaping and twirling with the best of them, though still invisible. '*Fouf*!' cried the princes as they bumped into empty air. And, '*Tish*!' cried the princesses as their goblets of wine seemed to vanish before they could drink them. But only the youngest was frightened. All the others laughed, and blamed the wine they'd drunk, and one another, and went on dancing, faster and faster, until the princes gasped for air and mercy, the princesses' coronets slipped and their shoes were in tatters, and the soldier felt as if, in one long magic night, he'd found and

lived the first part of the youth he'd lost.

And then the clock struck. *Ting*! *Ting*! *Ting*! Three o'clock! The flags were lowered and the candles snuffed, and the princesses hurried with their princes back to the lake. This time, out of pity for the youngest princess's partner, the soldier stepped in the boat of the eldest. And though they were among the first to leave the shore, by halfway over they were well behind.

'This is a strange thing,' the prince could not help remarking. 'I am more tired than a man should be. See how the others pull ahead.'

But the eldest princess simply smiled and comforted her straining oarsman: 'It always

seems to me that "well" and "quickly" seldom meet, and I am quite happy lying here.'

Yes, thought the soldier. She will make a fine match for a man with a grizzled beard like me.

As the boat reached the shore, the soldier leaped into the shallows and ran to overtake all the others. Some he passed in the first grove, some in the second, and some in the third. But by the time he reached the bottom of the stair-case, he was ahead of all of them. Up, up, up, he ran. And by the time the twelve tired princesses reached their room, his glittering branches were safely hidden under his shabby black cloak, and he was snoring in earnest.

'See?' said the eldest. 'Here's your old soldier, dreaming. Where are your worries now?' And she pulled the youngest sister's dress over her head for her, and hung it on a hook, and tucked her sleepy sister into bed, and threw her tattered shoes into the pile in the corner.

In the morning, the soldier woke and said to himself, 'These things I've seen are such great marvels that I will take my full three days to see them again.'

So all day he said nothing to the king or the grand vizier. And the next night, and the next, he followed the princesses down the dark staircase and through the glittering groves, and over the lake to the palace.

And there, like them, he danced till three o'clock – except that, in the strange magic of being invisible, he did not, like them, wear out his shoes. And when he was tired with dancing, he stole wine from one or another of the princesses' gold cups, and leaned back in some empty chair, and drank a toast to the old woman

in the dark wood, and listened to the fine music. On the second night, he told himself: 'Now I have had the second part of my lost youth.' And on the third: 'Now I have had it all, and will grow old content.' So, to remind himself of the splendour and ease and glory of these three special nights, as they left for the last time he took with him a golden cup he had stolen from under the eldest princess's hand when she stood up to dance.

On that third and last morning, the grand vizier rose with an even heavier heart than usual. He had enjoyed the company of the soldier, and didn't want to see him lose his head. So he dillied and dallied, until the king clapped his hands and ordered: 'Fetch in the man who claims he can tell me where my daughters go at night, and what they do.'

The twelve princesses crept along the passage in their bare feet to listen to what this snoring

fool would say. How pale their faces looked when the soldier unwrapped his shabby black cloak and out fell branches of silver and gold and diamonds, and a golden cup.

At the sight of these marvels, the grand vizier trembled with hope, and Nursie's heart lifted at the thought that she might never again have to hear the sad shuffle of footsteps down the tower stairs. Then the soldier stood fearlessly and told all who were listening where he had been and what he had seen. Each time he saw disbelief rising in their eyes, he pointed to the glittering branches and the golden cup.

The king was silent. Then he said, 'I will hear what my daughters have to say,' and sent Nursie to fetch them.

In they all trooped, the pretty ones giggling, the clever ones silent, and the youngest one peeping at her toes.

The king said to the eldest, 'Is it true what this soldier says about a magical palace under the earth, and lakes and princes and dancing?'

The eldest looked reproachfully at the soldier. But he looked firmly back at her. And some of the courage he'd brought back from her father's wars was in her own heart, too, because she stood fearlessly and told all who were listening,

'Yes. It is true.'

Then the king ordered the grand vizier to fetch the proclamation and told the soldier he must choose one of the twelve princesses for his wife.

Everyone's eyes crept to the youngest, for she was as rosy as the dawn. But the soldier remembered what the old woman had told him, and said cheerfully and wisely:

'I am no longer young, so I will choose the eldest. I am sure she and I will make a fine match.'

So they did, too. And when the old king died, the soldier took his place, and made an excellent ruler with the help of the grand vizier. He was kind to his sisters-in-law and built them a ballroom – nowhere near as fine as the other, but still excellent for dancing.

And the grand vizier grew his beard down to his feet.

And Nursie sat knitting peaceably for Samuel. And Sapphire. And Silas. And Serena. And Sidney. And Salome. And Septimus. And Sukie. And Stanley. And Sabrina. And Simon. And Baby Sappho, who kept peeping at her toes.

And the new king ordered the grand vizier to be sure there were no more wars in the old woman's corner of the kingdom. Or anywhere else, for that matter. So there were no more burned cottages, no more trampled crops. And every week, like clockwork, a basket was sent to her, filled to the brim with bread and eggs and meat and wine. So she was contented, too, in her dark wood, and thought it a very fine bargain for a shabby black cloak and a piece of advice, even if both were magic.

And everyone – everyone – danced every night of the week.

And they were all happy ever after.

Hansel and Gretel

Retold by Henrietta Branford

Illustrated by Lesley Harker

There was once a poor woodcutter who lived with his two young children and their stepmother on the edge of a great forest. I don't know his name, nor that of his wife, but the children's names were Hansel and Gretel.

At first the forest was all quiet mossy green below, with the soft rustle-bustle of the leaves above. But there came a summer when the sun shone hot and yellow day after day. Nice, you

might think. And so it was, at first. But by and by the streams turned to trickles and the ponds became puddles and the earth grew hard and cracked. Fields turned yellow and then brown. Animals died for want of a mouthful of grass. People, too, grew hungry and afraid.

The woodcutter could neither work nor sleep for worrying about his children. 'What can we do?' he asked his wife. 'We have no food, we have nothing for the children.'

'Go fishing,' said his wife. So he did. He caught the last little fish in the river. After that fish was gone, the family sat looking at the fish bones. The children would have liked to suck the bones, but, 'Go to bed, children,' snapped their stepmother. 'There's nothing more for you to eat.' She had half a loaf of mouldy bread hidden, but she meant to keep that for herself.

Hansel and Gretel went to bed hungry. When they had gone, their stepmother took the bones

from the pot and sniffed them. She looked at her husband. 'Two people could live for longer than four on the juice of these bones,' she said.

'Maybe so,' said her husband, 'but there are four of us.'

'Then the children must go,' said she.

'Never!' cried her husband. 'How can you think of such a thing?'

'Don't be so soft!' snapped his wife. 'We'll take them out into the forest, you can build them a fire and I will leave them half a crust I've got hidden. It's the only way.'

'No!' cried the woodcutter. 'Never! Nohow! That I will not do!'

'Do it, or we'll all be dead in a week,' hissed his wife. 'Do it if you love me.' And that's how she went on.

At last her husband agreed to do what she wanted. 'Good,' smiled his wife. 'I knew you'd see sense in the end. Come to bed now and be

cosy. Once it is done, you won't have to worry about them any more.'

Lying upstairs in their beds, Hansel and Gretel had heard every word. Hansel hopped out of bed and snuggled in beside his sister. 'Don't be afraid,' he said. 'I shall look after you. I know how to keep us both safe.' He crept downstairs, pulled on his jacket and peeped out at the moonlit garden. Everything in it was dead. Only the smooth white stones that lined the path shone milky white like pearls. Hansel picked up a pocketful and crept back to bed.

Early next morning the children's stepmother shook them awake. 'Get up!' she shouted.

'Get washed! Get dressed! We're off to cut wood in the forest.'

Their father picked up his axe and his saw. He wiped his eyes on his sleeve. Then he and his wife took Hansel and Gretel deep into the quiet green forest. They took them around and about, and around and about, until the children were quite lost. Every now and then Hansel hung back, looking over his shoulder.

'Why do you keep stopping, Hansel, and looking back towards the house?' asked his stepmother.

'I'm looking back to see my white cat,' Hansel answered. 'He's up on the roof of our house, saying goodbye to me.'

'Stupid boy,' snapped his stepmother, tugging his arm. 'That's not your white cat, it's just the morning sun shining on the chimney.'

Hansel didn't answer. He hadn't been looking at his white cat anyway. He had been laying

a trail with his smooth white stones to show him the way home.

By and by, when the children could walk no further, their father built them a fire of sticks and pine cones. 'Rest here and warm yourselves,' he said. 'We're going to cut wood. Stay by the fire, don't wander. The forest is a wicked place.'

'Come on,' said his wife. 'Hurry. It will soon be dark.' She gave the children a corner of crust. 'There'll be no more where that came from,' she told them. 'So don't eat it all at once.' Husband and wife hurried away under the trees.

The sun sank low and the forest grew dark, with here a rustle, there a bustle, here a sniff, there a snuff, and everywhere a patter. Hansel

and Gretel were very much afraid, but they lay down together by the fire and at last they slept.

When they woke up, the fire was out and the forest all around them was as dark as the inside of a cupboard. 'They've gone and left us all alone,' whispered Gretel.

'I know,' said Hansel. 'But I shall bring us both safe home. You'll see.'

When the moon sailed up into the sky, her beams lit up the round white stones like pearls on a string. Away ran Hansel and Gretel, down the pearly path to home, and got there just in time to find their stepmother finishing the fish-bone soup.

'Lazy, disobedient children!' she gasped. 'Why did you sleep so long by the fire?' Their father said nothing, but took them in his arms and held them close.

That night the children lay in their beds again, listening to their stepmother. 'This time there's

nothing left at all,' she said. 'Not so much as a fish bone. It's them or us. You know I'm right.'

'I'd rather we shared what we have, even if it's nothing, than take them back into the forest,' said her husband.

'That's stupid!' snapped his wife. 'How can you share nothing? Besides, you agreed to it the first time, so you must agree to it the second time.'

Upstairs in their beds, Hansel and Gretel heard it all. 'Don't worry, Gretel,' whispered Hansel. 'I'll keep us safe, just as I did before.' He crept from his bed and tiptoed downstairs. He put up his hand to lift the latch but the door would not open. His stepmother had locked it and hidden the key. Hansel crept back to bed.

Early next morning their stepmother shook the children up and out of bed. There was nothing but the end of a mouldy crust for breakfast.

'Don't eat it now, you'll want it later,' said their stepmother. And they set off once more, walking deep into the forest.

Again Hansel dawdled, looking back towards his home. 'What's the good of looking back, Hansel?' his stepmother asked. 'You know we must go on.'

'I'm looking at my pigeon,' said Hansel. 'He's up on our roof saying goodbye to me.'

'Daft boy!' scolded his stepmother. 'That's not your pigeon, it's the morning sun shining on the chimney-pot.'

Hansel didn't answer. He hadn't been looking at his pigeon anyway. He had been laying a trail of crumbs to show him the way home.

By and by they stopped, and their father built a fire. He told the children to wait while he went

off to cut wood. 'We'll be gone a good while,' he said. 'Remember that there are wild animals in the forest. Stay close to the fire.'

This time Hansel and Gretel were even more afraid, but at last they slept, lapped in the warmth of the burning embers. When they woke up, night shadows filled the forest. Wood shifted on the dying fire and sparks whirled up into the sky. An old hedgehog came up with a rustle and a snuffle, stopped to look at the two children, sitting so small and lonely under the stars, and trotted on. Soon it was quite dark. The children looked at one another.

'They've gone,' said Gretel. 'Haven't they?'

'I'm hungry,' said Hansel.

'I saved my corner of crust. I'll give you half if you like.'

'I used mine up to make us a trail of crumbs, Gretel. Wait till the moon comes out and then you'll see.'

But when the moon came out there was no trail of crumbs. Ants had carried them off. Birds had pecked them up. Lumbering black beetles had clicked their pincers and gobbled them down. They were gone.

Away went Hansel and Gretel, hand in hand, searching all the dark night for a way out of the forest. They walked all night and all the next day, but they could not find a path to lead them home.

By the end of the third day they were too tired to walk any further. They lay down together and shut their eyes. High above the branches, the moon looked down on them and smiled. But the

moon was not the only one out and about that night. A witch flew by on her broomstick, nosing here, sniffing there, searching for lost lonely travellers. She found the sleeping children and whispered a spell into their ears:

'Sleep on, pretty children, sleep,
In the magic forest deep,
You are hungry, I am too;
There's no one to take care of you.
Sleep on, pretty children, sleep,
In the magic forest deep.
When you wake up you will find
Sweets and treats of every kind,
Search for them and you will see;
Pretty children, come to me.'

When Hansel and Gretel woke up, they felt strange; very strange. 'There's something tugging at me,' said Gretel.

'I feel it too,' whispered Hansel. 'It's tugging at my hungriness.'

'Let's look for it,' said Gretel.

The children set off through the forest, drawn on close and tight by the witch's spell. By and by they came to a dear little house all made of chocolate and toffee and biscuits and sweets, with a roof of cake and a lawn of sugar frosting. There was a lollipop fence and a toffee-apple tree and a sweet soda fountain with a flock of ice-cream ducks. The children could hardly believe their luck.

The witch, too, was delighted. Up in the attic, where Hansel and Gretel could not see her, she

licked her lips. A black cat twined around her legs, mewing softly.

Hansel and Gretel ran towards the house. They couldn't wait to gulp down cake and sugar, to stuff their mouths with chocolate and toffee, to scoop up soda and lick up ice-cream ducks. Gretel broke off the flap of the letter-box and sat down to enjoy it.

Just as she sat down, a little creaking voice called out:

> *'Nibble, nibble, little mouse,*
> *Who is gnawing at my house?'*

Gretel put down her letter-box flap and answered bravely:

> *'It is not I, it is not I*
> *It is the wind, child of the sky.'*

And she took another bite.

The witch came down from the attic and poked her nose out of the door. When her black cat saw the children, he unsheathed his cruel claws and his cold green eyes shone like emeralds.

'Come in, my dears,' smiled the witch. 'Sit by my fire while I put food on the table and make up warm, soft beds. Come in, why not?'

Should they go in? No. Never! But, 'Thank you,' said Gretel. And, 'Yes please,' said Hansel. And in they went. The moment they stepped inside that house, chocolate and toffee disappeared, and all the biscuits and the sweets and the lollipop fence and the toffee-apple tree, the sweet soda fountain and the ice-cream ducks.

That house was made of nothing but sticks and mud. There was no food on the table and there were no warm beds. There was just a heap of rags beside an iron cage. Hansel and Gretel looked at the old woman. She didn't look kind any more. Too late, Hansel and Gretel understood. But before they could turn and run, the witch caught Hansel by the neck and bundled him into the cage and banged the door shut and locked it with an iron key.

'Get up!' she hissed at Gretel. 'Get up and get to work! I want a good cooked breakfast and I want it NOW! No, I want two – one for me and one for your brother. I shall soon fatten him up – and when he's fat enough I'll eat him!'

That's how it was. Hansel stayed locked in the cage and every day Gretel cooked porridge to fatten him up – but not one mouthful of it did she taste herself. No. The old woman gave her nothing but mouldy green bread. 'Your turn comes later,' she would say. 'After I've eaten your brother.' The black cat watched from his place by the fire, smiling a black cat smile.

Every morning the witch would rattle the bars of Hansel's cage. 'Stick your finger through the bars,' she'd say. 'Let me squeeze it. Are you getting fat?'

Every morning Hansel pushed out an old bone that he'd found on the floor of his cage. The witch, whose eyesight was very poor, would pinch the bone between her fingers, and frown, and shake her head. 'Gretel!' she'd shout. 'You're a rotten cook! Your brother is no more than skin and bone, there's not a decent mouthful on him!'

Gretel would cook more porridge. What else could she do? She was in the witch's power. And Hansel would eat it, though he hated porridge. He grew fat and slow, shut up in his cage.

Round about midnight every night, the witch would wake up her cat and call up her broomstick and go out and away, locking the door behind her. While she was gone, Gretel would search for the iron key that might unlock her brother. She even searched the witch's bedroom. There was a great high bed made of bones and a pumpkin head beside it with a candle for a light. It seemed to be laughing at Gretel. Old clothes, odd shoes, and pairs of spectacles spilled out from under the bed. Gretel would search as best she could but the key didn't want to be found. At last she would sit down next to Hansel's cage. They would hold hands through the bars and do their best to comfort one another. 'I'll find it in the end, Hansel, I know I will,'

Gretel would promise. 'And when I do, we'll run away together.'

Time passed in the dark house, slow as sorrow, until one dark and stormy night, the witch called up her cat as usual, mounted her broomstick and away they went, skimming over the treetops, weaving through the thickets, poking into hollow places, sniffing and spying for lost lonely travellers.

Back in the house, the fire went out. The room grew pitchy dark. Gretel crept out from under her rags. She lit a candle and she searched the whole house but still she found no key. By and by she pressed herself to Hansel's cage. The children leaned close and held each other's hands

tight, tight against the dark.

'It's now or never, Gretel,' whispered Hansel.
'You must run away tonight. The witch is hungry for me, I can tell. She won't wait much longer.
Go now, tonight. Go quickly before she comes
back!'

'Where would I run to, without you, Hansel?'

'Anywhere. There can't be a worse place than
this.'

'What about you, Hansel?'

'I must stay here and face what's coming to
me.'

'Not on your own, though. Never on your
own. We'll face what comes together.'

Then came a thumping and bumping from up
on the roof. 'Too late, Gretel,' whispered Hansel.
'Quick – into bed.' Gretel crept under her pile
of rags and shut her eyes just as the witch slid
down the chimney and into the room, shaking
the soot from her hair. She had caught nothing

and nobody all night and she was tired and hungry.

She went to Hansel's cage and rattled the bars. Hansel pushed the old bone out for her to feel: it was just as thin as ever. 'Wake up, Gretel!' shouted the witch. 'Wake up, you ugly waste of space! Your brother hasn't gained so much as a slick or a sliver of fat! Get up and light the fire! Heat up the oven! Today we'll cook him, fat or thin!'

Gretel could hardly see to light the fire, she cried so hard. But she lit it just the same. What else could she do? And Hansel watched her, knowing what the fire was for. By and by the logs glowed red and the old brick oven grew hot and

the witch, thinking of the feast to come, grew hungry.

'*One* may not be enough,' she said to her black cat. '*Two* would certainly be better.' The black cat licked his lips. 'Gretel,' said the witch, 'lean into the oven and tell me if it's hot enough.'

'Yes, Auntie,' said Gretel. And she peeped in. 'I think it's hot enough,' she said, 'but there's something sitting in there, right at the back of the oven. What can it be?'

'Out of my way, stupid, and let me look,' shouted the witch.

'Certainly, Auntie, right away,' said Gretel. '*You* lean in and have a look.'

The moment the witch leaned in, Gretel gave her an almighty shove. In went the witch, slam bang into her own oven. Gretel shut the oven door tight and stood beside it, shaking.

Well, that was the end of the witch. It was the end of the black cat too: he turned to soot and cinders

and floated up the chimney. And there, right where he'd been sitting, lay the key to the cage. Gretel picked it up and slid it into the lock. She turned it carefully. The door swung open with a groan and out jumped Hansel, into Gretel's arms. They hugged and they hugged and they hugged one another. Then they sat down to think.

'All witches have hidden treasure,' Hansel said, when he had thought enough. 'Let's look for hers.' The children tipped up boxes, swept crockery crashing off shelves, tore down curtains, ripped up clothes, threw spell books to burn on the fire, and sent potions and lotions swirling away in a sticky black pall of smoke that blotted out the sky – but only for a moment.

When the whole house was in a fine mess and muddle, Hansel's eye fell on the witch's coal box. He kicked it over with the toe of his boot and out rolled the coal, all over the carpet. And after the coal, something else. Something shiny – a big old silver box. Gretel took a knife and prised it open.

That box was *stuffed* with gold and silver coins, with rings and earrings and necklaces and jewels of all kinds, taken from the ears and the fingers and the pockets of all the people the witch had eaten, down all the many hundred years she'd lived in that dark house. There were diamonds and rubies, emeralds, sapphires, blood red coral and milky white pearls. There was even a little jewelled watch, still ticking softly.

The children filled their pockets with treasures of every kind. Then away they ran, hand in hand under the rustling leaves. When they stopped to look back, the witch's house was gone. All that remained was a little pile of ashes. Foxgloves

were already growing through them, green against the grey.

After a mile or two, Hansel and Gretel came to a rushing river. 'I'm sure our home is on the other side,' said Hansel. 'But how can we cross over?'

'Someone will help us,' said Gretel.

No sooner had she spoken than two white swans came swimming up-river with the water lap-lapping and the soft foam curling round their breast feathers.

'Father Swan, Mother Swan, we need to cross the river. Will you help us?' Gretel asked.

The swans looked at Gretel out of their wise black eyes. They nodded their sleek heads and

spoke to one another in swan language, which is silent. Then they swam to the bank and waited while the children climbed on to their backs.

When they reached the far bank, Hansel and Gretel thanked the swans politely and set off to search for home.

By and by the forest began to look familiar. Hansel and Gretel began to run. Before long they could see their father's house away in the distance. They pelted down the path and through the garden, right to their own front doorstep. The door stood open. There at the table sat their father, carving a piece of wood into the likeness of his two lost children.

When he looked up and saw Hansel and Gretel standing in the doorway, he smiled the first smile he'd smiled since the dreadful day he left them alone in the forest. It was the biggest, longest smile he'd ever smiled.

Hansel and Gretel jumped into his arms. When

they had finished hugging, they emptied their pockets out on to the kitchen table. There lay the treasure, shining in the sunlight. It wasn't magic and it didn't disappear. But what about their cruel stepmother? Well, she wasn't there any more. At the very same moment when the witch died in the forest, so did the wicked stepmother.

And what happened next? Well, Hansel and Gretel and their father lived happily ever after – and they were never hungry again. And that's all that I can tell you.

Rapunzel

Retold by Jacqueline Wilson
Illustrated by Nick Sharratt

There was once a husband and wife who longed for a child. The man made a cradle out of oak and carved buttercups and daisies round the side. The woman sewed many silk outfits and embroidered flocks of lovebirds and butterflies on every single baby garment.

The years went by. The cradle gathered dust in a corner because the woman couldn't bear to go near it. The baby clothes stayed shut in a drawer,

the bright birds and butterflies trapped in the dark.

The husband hoped his wife might accept her lot as she grew older but if anything her longing grew worse. Sometimes he saw her fold her arms and rock them as if she were holding an invisible baby. He couldn't stand seeing her aching so badly.

The couple lived in a cottage at the edge of the village. The very last house was a forbidding dark dwelling with dragons painted on the door and a glowering griffin weathervane on the roof. The garden was surrounded by a high wall but the husband and wife could peep down into it when they were upstairs in their cottage.

It was no ordinary garden of cornflowers and cabbages. They recognized some of the plants, lavender, mint, camomile, foxglove . . . but there were many strange herbs they'd never seen before.

They rarely spied their neighbour, a wild-looking old woman with tangled grey hair and stark black clothing. She sold herbal remedies and acted as a midwife – but most of the villagers shunned her, whispering that she was a witch. One stupid small boy dared torment her, climbing her wall and pulling up some of her plants. That night he had a fit, fell into a trance, and never walked or talked again.

The husband and wife steered well clear of their neighbour – but the husband couldn't help wondering if she might have some magic potion that could help them have a child. She was a midwife, after all. She might know some special secrets.

97

One morning the wife discovered a strand of grey in her fair hair. She started weeping because she knew she was almost too old to have a baby now. The sound of her sobs spurred the husband on.

He walked out of the cottage, down the garden path, out of his wooden gate – and through the sharply spiked iron arch belonging to his neighbour. He stood still in the strange garden, staring all around him. The cobbled path seemed to tilt first one way, then the other, making him dizzy. He forced himself towards the house, plants brushing against his ankles with their bristly leaves, creepers coiling round his calves as if they had a life of their own.

It took him all his courage to seize the leering

lion's-head knocker. It was horribly hot to the touch so that he only dared one timid rap before snatching his hand away. The door opened almost immediately. The bent old woman stood before him, squinting up at him from behind her grey hanks of hair.

'I'm so sorry to disturb you, Madam,' the husband said. 'It's just that I couldn't help wondering . . . You seem so learned in matters of magic . . .' His voice tailed away.

The old woman waited, rubbing her dry old hands together so that they made a rasping noise.

'It's my wife,' the husband continued desperately. 'She's always longed for a child and now I'm so scared this longing is driving her demented. Is there any way at all you can help? Some pill, some potion, some secret spell? I'm not a rich man but I'd be willing to give you all my savings – a purse of gold – if you will help us.'

The old woman's mouth tightened until

her dry lips disappeared.

'I have always longed for a daughter myself,' she said, her old eyes watering.

The husband stared at her in astonishment, amazed that a weird old witch woman could want a child.

'Do not look so surprised,' she said bitterly. She sniffed and composed herself. 'However, you have been courteous. I do know a few secret tricks that might work.' She whispered in his ear. 'And make your wife a special rapunzel salad tonight.'

'Rapunzel?' said the husband.

'You might call it rampion. It's a salad delicacy.'

'We haven't got any rampion in our vegetable garden. Would lettuce do instead?' said the husband.

'It won't do at all,' said the old woman. 'Here, I have a special rampion patch myself. I will pick you a bunch. But I can only spare you a little.'

'It's very kind of you to spare me any,' said the husband gratefully. 'What do I owe you?' He rather hoped she wasn't going to charge him too many pieces of gold for a couple of tips and a bunch of green leaves.

'You don't owe me anything, neighbour. But do not come back and trouble me again,' said the old woman, and she shut her door.

The husband went back to his wife and told her he'd consulted with the old woman. She was impressed by his courage, but did not think the witch's tricks would work – though she ate all her rampion salad supper with great relish.

Weeks passed. The husband and wife dared

start hoping. Months passed. The wife's gown grew tight around her waist. She clasped her rounded stomach, her face soft with joy.

'I am going to have a baby!' she said.

The husband put his arms around his dear wife and they both wept with happiness.

The wife was not very well during the months she carried her child. She had to rest in her bed many days and she was often sick.

'You must eat something, my love. You have to nourish our baby as well as yourself,' said the husband.

'I can't fancy any food at all – except that strange rampion,' said the wife. 'Oh, I so long for

that sweet delicious fresh tangy taste. Can't you ask the old witch for some more?'

'She said she could only spare me a little. And she warned me not to trouble her again.' The husband hesitated. 'But I could try telling her just how much it would mean to you.'

So he went round to the old woman. She glared at him when she opened her door. He told her his wife was now with child and begged for another bunch of rampion.

'I told you, I cannot spare you any more.'

'She craves the taste so.'

'Then she must go on craving,' said the old woman sharply. 'I'm warning you! You will bitterly regret it if you disturb me again.'

The wife wept when told of the old woman's refusal. She sat up in bed all day and half the night, looking down into the garden where she could see the green rampion patch. Her stomach was still round, but her face grew pale and

pinched and the flesh fell away from her arms and legs. The husband was tormented with this new worry, scared his wife would not survive her pregnancy.

He knew there was no point begging the old woman once more. He decided to take matters into his own hands. He knew what he had to do.

He waited until long past midnight when the moon was hidden by clouds. Then he crept out of his house in his stockinged feet. The iron arch was locked but he climbed up and over it, though hidden spikes tore great grooves in his hands. He sucked his bloody fingers and stumbled up and down the cobbled path, trying to locate the rampion patch. A huge creeper wound itself right round his neck like a cobra and gave him such a shock he fell headlong. He lay stunned for a moment – and then realized he had fallen right into the rampion patch.

He plucked as many leaves as he could,

scrambled to his feet, and was just stumbling back to the gate when he heard the front door open.

The moon came out, a huge pearly full moon that cast an eerie silver glow upon the garden. The old woman stood right in front of him, her eyes glittering, her face contorted, her mouth open. Her few teeth were filed into points. She looked as if she could tear out his throat with one bite.

'How dare you steal from me!' she shrieked.

'Oh please, have mercy! I know I shouldn't have tried – but my wife is so ill and craves your rampion so very badly, you have no idea.'

'Yes, I have no idea,' said the old woman,

hugging her bent old body tight with her crooked hands.

'Can't you take pity on us?' the husband begged. 'If my wife cannot eat your rampion she will surely die.'

The old woman said nothing for a long, long while. A little trickle of saliva slid from between her pointed teeth and dribbled down her chin. Her eyes gleamed like a wild cat's. The husband wondered whether to try to make a run for it but his sodden feet seemed planted in her garden and he could scarcely move a muscle. He realized he was under a terrible enchantment.

'Please, I beg you, have mercy!' he gasped. 'I will do anything, give you anything, if you will let me go back to my wife.'

'Anything at all?' said the old woman.

'Anything at all,' the husband repeated desperately. 'I swear it.'

'Then your wife shall have all the rampion she

can eat,' said the old woman, stooping down and gathering great fistfuls of it. She thrust them at the husband, who found he could wrench his feet free again. 'But, in return . . .'

He waited, heart thudding.

The old woman raised her head and pointed a shaking finger.

'In return . . . If your wife has a daughter you must give the child to me.'

The husband gasped and implored but the old woman turned her back on him and shut herself into her dark house.

He took the rampion back to his ailing wife. She seized it joyously, eating it straight from his

hand, not even bothering to wash the earth away.

'Thank the Lord the old witch didn't catch you!' she said.

The husband didn't dare tell her what had happened. He could not stand to worry her so. Besides, they might well have a son.

He consulted all the other old women in the village to see if they had any way of divining the sex of the unborn child. His wife laughed as they dandled rings on ribbons above her swollen stomach.

'I don't care whether our baby is a boy or a girl,' she said.

'I care,' said the husband. He shut his eyes as if he were praying. 'It has to be a boy.'

'It will be a boy,' cried the old women as the ring swung backwards and forwards.

'A baby boy,' said the wife, and she sounded pleased.

She looked so much better, a pink flush to her

cheek. She bloomed throughout the rest of her pregnancy like a sweet round peach. The husband grew thin and pale with dread.

'It has to be a boy,' he muttered, his hands on the wife's stomach.

He could feel the baby kicking within.

'My son,' he whispered.

'Our son,' said the wife.

But it wasn't a son. The wife had an easy labour and gave birth to a beautiful blonde daughter.

'A girl!' said the husband, and burst into tears.

'Our daughter,' said the wife.

'My daughter,' said the old witch-woman, suddenly appearing in the room as if she had leaped through the window. She seized hold of the newborn child, still pink and naked, and held her tight against her sunken chest.

'No!' screamed the wife, trying to get out of bed, but stuck fast.

'No!' shouted the husband, reaching out his arms, but able to grasp nothing.

'Yes,' said the old woman, wrapping the baby in a blanket and cradling her. 'She is my daughter now and I name her Rapunzel.' She looked over at the anguished wife. 'Do not worry, I will be a loving mother to the child.'

'My child,' the wife gasped.

'Mine now,' said the old woman. 'But perhaps fate will still be kind to you and grant you another. Eat my rampion whenever you wish. I am going to be far, far away.'

And with that she wrapped her cloak around herself and the child . . . and vanished.

The old woman set up home in another village the other end of the country. She laid out another elaborate herb garden and sewed it with many seeds – but no rampion. She looked after Rapunzel with loving care, singing to the child at night, telling her magical stories, teaching her the names of all the herbs and how to turn them into potions and remedies. She did not send Rapunzel to the village school when she was five. She taught the child to read and write herself.

The old woman and Rapunzel kept very much to themselves, but as the girl grew older children came calling every day, desperate to see and talk and play with the strange little girl with such old-fashioned sweet manners and such amazing hair. Rapunzel was a bonnie baby and a pretty little girl but by the time she got to eleven it was obvious she was growing into a stunning beauty. She had a lovely face and a lithe form but the most wondrous thing about her was her hair. It

was thick and blonde with a natural wave. The old woman washed it with special herbal shampoo and brushed it a hundred strokes each night with an ivory-backed bristle brush. Rapunzel's hair grew long and strong and shining. It was down past her shoulders by the time she was two, curling at her waist by five, gently brushing the backs of her knees at eight, and now at eleven Rapunzel's hair swept the floor like a golden train.

Of course this was scarcely practical, so during the day the old woman braided it, her shaking fingers surprisingly nimble as she plaited each heavy silken strand, and then she looped the braids up so that Rapunzel had her own golden halo of hair. It was so heavy on her head that it was always a great relief to untie it all at bedtime. The old woman would sometimes plunge her hands into its warmth or delicately finger one little curl. Once she felt her own

sparse grey straggles and sighed.

'I expect you had long golden hair when you were little, Mother,' said Rapunzel. 'But anyway, I think grey hair is very distinguished.'

'You are a sweet child, daughter,' said the old woman. 'You do love me, don't you, Rapunzel?'

'More than anyone in the world, Mother,' said Rapunzel.

'And you never feel you'd be happier living anywhere else?'

'I only ever want to live with you,' said Rapunzel.

There was a knock on the door at that moment. Half a dozen ragged boys from the village had come to call on Rapunzel. The old woman sent them away curtly. A few days later a young nobleman from a nearby castle came to see this girl with the wondrous hair for himself. The old woman sent him away with equal abruptness. The next day three more

young men came calling.

'Do we have to send them all away, Mother?' said Rapunzel. 'It might be pleasant to have company from time to time.'

'We are company. We don't need anyone else,' said the old woman gruffly.

The callers became such a problem as Rapunzel's hair grew to ever more fabulous golden lengths that the old woman became desperate. She worked her magical powers to the ultimate and then woke Rapunzel very early on her twelfth birthday and told her she had an astonishing present for her. She said it was hidden deep in the forest.

'Why did you hide it away there, Mother?' asked Rapunzel.

'So that no one else will see it. It's our very own special secret,' said the old woman, taking Rapunzel by the hand.

They walked far into the dark forest. Rapunzel couldn't help being a little frightened, especially when an animal snarled in the distance or a bird suddenly soared in the air, almost entangling itself in Rapunzel's abundant tresses.

'Are we nearly there, Mother?'

'Very nearly, my dear,' said the old woman.

She held Rapunzel's hand very tightly indeed. The trees suddenly thinned and they stepped into a sunlit round clearing edged by tall protective oaks. Skylarks spiralled high in the air above, squirrels scampered in the grass below. At the very centre of the clearing was a shining golden tower.

Rapunzel stood still, dazzled.

'What is this beautiful tower, Mother?'

'It's a new home, daughter dearest,' said the old woman.

'Our new home?' said Rapunzel.

'Your new home, Rapunzel,' said the old woman.

She pointed to the tower. It shone so strongly in the sunlight that Rapunzel had to hide her eyes. The light seared her very eyelids and she had to crouch down, her arms over her head. She seemed to be whirled around, up and up and up . . . and then suddenly she found herself curled on the floor. She wasn't lying on the grass in the sunlight. She was crouching on dark red carpet.

Rapunzel lifted her head and stared all around her. She was in a round red chamber, a beautiful room with velvet couches and crimson tapestries and ruby glass lamps. There was a table set with all her favourite dishes, a chest of beautiful dresses all colours of the rainbow, a shelf of all

her special childhood toys. There was a bed with a deep rose coverlet and a pink satin pillow, a dressing table set with her own ivory-backed hairbrush.

'My home?' Rapunzel whispered. And then she shouted, 'Mother? Mother, where are you? *Mother*!'

'Come to the window, Rapunzel,' the old woman called.

Rapunzel picked herself up and ran to the one high-up window in the room. She peered down . . . and there was the old woman far below.

'Mother! Why have you shut me up in the tower alone?' Rapunzel screamed.

'I have to keep you safe, my darling,' the old

woman said. 'Don't be afraid. You will be so happy in your special tower. I will come and visit you every single day. I will bring you fresh food and brush your beautiful hair and tell you stories and sing you to sleep.'

'But how will you get in? There's no door to the chamber, no way into the tower,' said Rapunzel.

'It will be simple, my child. I shall call up to you, "Rapunzel, Rapunzel, let down your long hair," and you will let down your wondrous long hair braided into a rope. It will reach nearly to the ground. I will climb up and be with you,' said the old woman. 'That's how I will get in.'

'But . . . how will I get out?' said Rapunzel.

The old woman did not answer. Rapunzel realized she was trapped.

She spent weeks trying to work out a way to escape. If she jumped straight out of the window she would be dashed to death. She stared at the

tiny squirrels far down below. She couldn't climb down because the golden bricks were smooth as glass. She looked up at the skylarks above and wished she had wings.

She examined every inch of her deep red room, pulling up the carpet, wrenching the heavy cupboard from the wall, but she could not find a crack or a chink anywhere. There was no sign of a way out. She was trapped, trapped, trapped.

Every day the old woman would come and call, 'Rapunzel, Rapunzel, let down your long hair.'

Rapunzel would throw down her massive braid and the old woman would haul herself up and up and up, through the window and into

Rapunzel's chamber. She brought Rapunzel a new present every day – another beautiful gown, a phial of perfume, a story book, a singing bird in a cage. Sometimes Rapunzel was grateful and hugged the old woman and they had happy times together. Sometimes Rapunzel was restless and resentful.

'I don't want your presents. I don't want you. Just let me out!' she screamed, and she tore her gown and spilt the perfume and threw the book out of the window and let the bird out of its cage to fly free.

But after a while Rapunzel stopped rebelling. She went about her daily tasks in a dream. She behaved in a kindly way to the old woman, but with no feeling. Every evening by herself she watched the sun set and sang a sad sweet lament as the blue sky became as red as her own room.

One evening a prince lost his way as he rode through the forest. His horse stumbled into the clearing. The prince was surprised by the golden tower – and when he heard the sweet song the hair stood up on the back of his neck. He got down from his horse and went round and round the tower, looking for the way in. The song went on and on up above, and he felt desperate to see the singer. But there was no way in and he eventually gave up and rode away.

He came back to the clearing every evening, utterly enchanted by the sweetness and sadness of the song, nearly driven demented by his desire. He came earlier and earlier. One day he came so early he saw the old woman stumbling along

towards the tower. He hid behind one of the oaks and watched her crane her neck and call up, 'Rapunzel, Rapunzel, let down your long hair.'

He held his breath as a great golden rope of hair tumbled down from the high window. He watched as the old woman clambered upwards, up and up and up – and in the window. The hair was withdrawn. He waited and watched a long time. Eventually the golden rope was thrown out and the old woman wobbled her way down and down its fabulous length until her old pointed boots touched the grass. He let her hobble off out of sight.

He waited, his heart racing, his fists clenched. Then he approached the foot of the tower, craned his neck, and called up in a cracked, old-woman voice, 'Rapunzel, Rapunzel, let down your long hair.'

The amazingly long strong braid of hair swung down out of the window. The prince seized it

eagerly, marvelling at its warm silkiness, and
started climbing up and up and up . . . and in at
the window.

Rapunzel screamed as he jumped into the
midst of her chamber. She tried to run, but she'd
wound her hair round a hook at the window to
relieve the strain on her scalp and she was caught
fast.

'Allow me,' said the Prince, and he deftly
unhooked her and helped her haul her hair back
up into the room.

Rapunzel wrapped her plait around herself in
her anxiety.

'I thought you were Mother returning. Where
is she? You haven't harmed her?'

'Of course not, Madam.'

'Who are you? You're not one of the boys from
the village?'

The Prince stood up straight, displaying his
courtly clothes.

'I am a Prince,' he informed her. 'And you must be an enchanted Princess, shut up in this golden tower.'

'I'm not a Princess. I'm only Rapunzel,' she said, giggling.

'You're a Princess to me,' said the Prince, and he took her hand and kissed it.

He stayed very late that night. He came the next day, after the old woman had paid her visit. He stayed even later. He came every evening at sunset, courting his beautiful Rapunzel – and now he did not leave until sunrise. He loved Rapunzel with all his heart and soul and she loved him too, deeply and passionately.

'How can I carry you away, my darling Rapunzel? I want to take you to my Palace and make you my real Princess,' said the Prince, stroking the long shimmering waterfall of her hair. 'You're so beautiful. Your hair is so strong and yet it's so silky too.'

Rapunzel started. 'Skeins of silk!' she said. 'That's it. Bring me a skein of silk every time you visit me, dearest Prince. I will braid them tight and strong so that they make a ladder. When the ladder is long enough I will tie it to the window hook and climb down from the tower into your arms.'

It seemed a splendid plan. The Prince did as she suggested and brought a skein of silk every day. Rapunzel spent hours every day constructing the silken ladder. It was good to have something to do with her time. Since the Prince started visiting her she had grown bored with all her old child-ish games. She could not even amuse herself

dressing up in all her rainbow gowns because many of them did not fit her any more. Even the loosest purple gown was growing tighter and tighter at the waist.

The old woman seemed to be growing smaller and frailer as Rapunzel grew bigger and more bonnie. She had difficulty clambering up the rope of Rapunzel's hair. Rapunzel had to reach out when she got to the window to haul her in.

One morning the effort was so great that the taut seams on her purple gown couldn't take the strain any more. As she pulled the old woman into her chamber Rapunzel's dress tore almost in two and slithered about her thickening waist. The old woman stared at her soft new curves and gave a great howl of realization.

'You are going to have a child!' she gasped.

Rapunzel was very frightened – and yet in the midst of her fear and anxiety a deep happiness made her blush.

'I am going to have the Prince's baby!' she said. 'Oh, how wonderful!'

'You wicked deceitful ungrateful girl! You are no longer my daughter,' screamed the old woman.

She seized a pair of sharp scissors and cut her way straight through Rapunzel's wonderful plait, sawing it right off at the nape of her neck. Then she took the girl and shook her hard until the red chamber whirled all around her and Rapunzel's eyes rolled up and she fell down down down into darkness . . .

When she awoke she was alone in a barren desert. She put her poor shorn head on her knees and wept.

The old woman stayed hidden in Rapunzel's tower. Towards sunset the Prince came eagerly to meet up with his love.

'Rapunzel, Rapunzel, let down your long hair,' he called.

The witch took Rapunzel's cut-off braid,

secured one end to the window hook and let the golden plait slither down to the ground. The Prince climbed up and up and up, and put one leg over the window ledge – and then stopped dead, staring at the old woman in front of him, her face contorted with rage.

'Where is Rapunzel?' he gasped.

'She is gone – and you will never see her again,' the old woman screamed.

She pushed the Prince hard so that he fell back out of the window, down and down and down. Thorn bushes suddenly sprouted out of the green grass. The Prince landed in these thorns and was almost torn to pieces. Two big thorns pierced his

eyes so that he could no longer see.

He stumbled off in this new dark world, calling for Rapunzel.

He felt his way right through the forest and journeyed to and fro across the land, blindly searching for his lost love. A year went by, and then another. Time had no meaning for the Prince. He knew he had to search for Rapunzel to the end of his days.

But then, one evening when there was a beautiful blood-red sunset (though of course he couldn't see it) the Prince heard the sweetest saddest singing. It was very soft and far away – but unmistakable.

'Rapunzel!' he said, and he started running, stumbling and tapping his stick before him frantically.

Rapunzel stopped singing for an instant, hearing his dear voice calling her name.

'My Prince?' she said, and she ran out of the

makeshift hovel that was now her home.

She saw a blind man in rags staggering towards her – but knew at once who he was.

'My Prince!' she cried, tears of joy rolling down her cheeks.

'Rapunzel!' cried the Prince. He threw away his stick and held out his arms.

Rapunzel ran right into his embrace. Her tears fell on his wounded eyes, washing out the deeply embedded thorns. The Prince could see again. He saw his own beloved Rapunzel, her hair now growing way past her shoulders. He also saw the rosy-cheeked fair twins tumbling outdoors to meet their father for the first time.

The Prince took his family back to his Kingdom where they lived happily ever after.

The distraught old witch-woman wandered the world but ended up back in her original old cottage with dragons on the door and the griffin weathervane on the roof. Rapunzel's parents had

moved away, but the villagers said the wife had given birth to a fine son a year after she lost her daughter.

A new husband and wife lived in their cottage. They had no children. One night the old woman heard noises coming from the garden and found the husband in her rampion patch . . .

Aesop's Fables

Retold by Malorie Blackman

Illustrated by Patrice Aggs

Foxy and the Sour Grapes

Foxy was walking along the dusty road one day, minding his own business and thinking foxy thoughts, when he came across a high vine. Now this vine was laden down with big, beckoning grapes.

'My! You look juicy. You look sweet! You look good enough to eat,' said Foxy, licking his lips.

So up he hopped, he jumped, he leaped. But he just couldn't reach those grapes. He took a running jump at them. He bounced. He vaulted.

He sprang. But nothing doing.

Slinking away, Foxy had a growl, a scowl, a glower. He said, 'I bet those grapes are yuck and sour!'

Some people comfort themselves by pretending that they don't want what they can't have or can't get.

The Sun and the North Wind

'When you get right down to it, I'm stronger than you,' said the North Wind.

'You really think so?' smiled the Sun.

'All right then, I'll prove it,' said the North Wind. 'You see that man down there with a coat

on? I bet I can blow his coat right off. Watch this!'

And the North Wind blew and Blew and BLEW. He blew around the man's head, around his legs, around his back and his chest, trying to tear his coat off. But the man just pulled his coat even more firmly around him, shivering against the cold.

'D'you mind if I have a try?' said the Sun.

And he shone. Warm, soft, golden rays.

'What funny peculiar weather!' said the man, unbuttoning his coat.

And the Sun shone some more. Bright, light rays everywhere.

'I'm melting,' the man gasped. And he pulled off his coat and slung it over his shoulder.

'I win! I win!' grinned the Sun. 'Deal with that!'

Persuasion is always better than force.

The Tortoise and the Hare

'Tortoise, you are so slow! How can you stand it?' asked the Hare.

'I like my pace. I have time to admire the sky and the flowers and listen to the breeze blow.'

'Phooey!' Hare snorted. 'When I run I get to where I'm going almost before I leave!'

Oh, for goodness' sake,' Tortoise said. 'Speed isn't everything. I bet if we had a race right here and now, I'd have a good chance of beating you. How about a race over the hill and back?'

Hare roared with laughter. 'You and me have a race? You wouldn't stand a chance.'

'We'll see.' Tortoise smiled.

But Hare didn't reply. He'd already started running. It wasn't long before Hare was way, way out in front.

'Why am I hurrying? That tortoise is so slow,

I could run this race fifteen times before he's even finished once. I might as well take it easy.' So Hare settled down for a nap. 'I can have a little sleep and still beat that tortoise – easy peasy, lemon squeezy!' And he closed his eyes and started snoring.

A little while later, the tortoise plodded past the sleeping hare and continued on his way, over the hill and back again. Hare awoke and raced to catch up but he'd left it too late. Tortoise crossed the finish line first and beat him.

Slowly but surely often wins the race. Focus and concentration will often bring success where natural talent but no determination will not.

The Lion and the Fox

An old lion came up with a plan to get himself some food without having to run and sweat and work for it. He lay in a cave and moaned and groaned for all he was worth.

'Ooh, my head hurts. Ooh, my back aches. Ooh, my paws are so sore. I'm ill! I'm sick! I'm dying!'

It wasn't long before animal after animal came to see how the poor lion was doing. But the moment they entered the lion's cave, he pounced on them and gobbled them up.

One day a fox came to call. He stood outside the cave and asked, 'How are you, Lion? Feeling better?'

'Not at all,' croaked the lion. 'Come in and see for yourself.'

'I would,' said the wise fox, 'if it wasn't for the

140

fact that I can see plenty of tracks going into your cave and not a single one coming out again!'

Look before you leap.

The Lion and the Man

A lion and a man were travelling along a road together. They started arguing about which one of them was the stronger, the more powerful. They came across a statue at the side of the road – a statue of a man strangling a lion with his bare hands.

'You see that!' said the man. 'That just proves my point. Over there is a statue of a man over-powering a lion.'

The lion smiled a wry, dry smile. 'If lions bothered to carve and sculpt, I'm sure you'd see a lot of statues of lions with humans under their paws.'

> *Each person who describes an event can't help but put his or her own slant on it. We all believe our own point of view is more true than anyone else's.*

The Ants and the Grasshopper

It was summer. And while the ants gathered seeds and nuts for the cold days to come, grasshopper jumped about and sang happily in the sun. But summer didn't last for ever. Winter came. It blew cold and hard and fierce.

Poor grasshopper was starving. There was no food anywhere. Dying of hunger and cold, he made his way to the ants and begged them for something to eat.

'And what were you doing in summer while we were working hard to gather up all this food?' the ants asked.

'I was singing,' the grasshopper replied.

'Really!' said the ants, less than impressed. 'Well, as you sang then, you can dance now – and see where that gets you.'

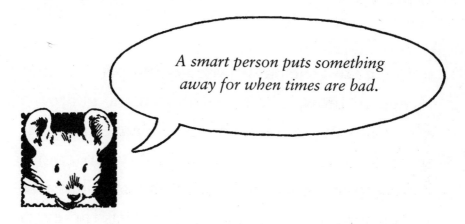

A smart person puts something away for when times are bad.

The Wolf's Dinner

A wolf waited until the goatherd went away to have his dinner and then he pounced. He caught up a kid in his powerful jaws and turned to run away and devour his catch in private.

'Wait a moment,' said the kid. 'I know you're going to eat me, but I have also heard that you play the flute more sweetly than any other animal alive. I'm sure if you were to play now, many more of my family would willingly follow you.'

So the wolf picked up the goatherd's flute and started to blow. The noise alerted the goatherd who came back with help and drove the wolf away.

'Serve me right,' said the wolf as he ran off. 'I'm a butcher. I had no business being a musician as well.'

*If you stick
to what you do well, success
will surely follow.*

The Vixen and the Lioness

'Really! Is that all you could manage?!' scoffed the vixen. 'Look at my lovely cubs. I have loads! Five beautiful cubs. You only have a measly one.'

'Only one,' came the reply. 'But a lion.'

*Quality,
not quantity,
is what counts.*

The Dog and the Bone

A dog stole a juicy bone and ran off with it in his mouth. He came to a calm river where, looking down, he was surprised to see another dog staring back at him. This other dog also had a bone in his mouth, but the other dog's bone looked much more meaty and juicy.

'Give me that bone. It's mine!' the first dog growled. And he lunged for it.

As his own bone fell into the river and was swept away, too late the dog realized that he had been growling at his own reflection.

Being too greedy can often lose you what you already have.

At Dinner with Stork and Fox

Fox invited the stork over for dinner. He served delicious soup in a wide, flat soup bowl. Try as she might, Stork couldn't pick up a drop in her long beak, much less swallow anything.

'Not eating, Stork?' asked Fox, enjoying himself. 'Here! Let me help.'

And Fox licked up Stork's portion as well. Poor Stork had to go home hungry but she was determined to get her own back. The following week, Stork invited Fox to dinner.

'I'm cooking loads, so come hungry,' said Stork.

Ravenous, Fox sat down to dinner. He could smell wonderful smells coming from Stork's kitchen.

'I've cooked one of your favourites,' said Stork.

And in she came with two long, thin pitchers of stew.

'Eat up!' said Stork, dipping her beak into the pitcher and eating her fill.

But try as he might, the fox couldn't get a bite. He couldn't get his snout into the thin pitcher.

'Not hungry? Here! Let me help you,' said Stork. And she ate Fox's portion as well, as he slunk back home with his tail between his legs.

If you are spiteful to others, you shouldn't be surprised when they are spiteful to you.

The Lion, the Fox and the Donkey

One day a lion, a fox and a donkey went hunting. After a hard day's work, they had caught and killed a number of animals.

'Now then,' said the lion to the donkey. 'If you will divide up the food, we can each take our share and go home.'

The donkey divided the food into three equal portions. But when the lion saw this, in a rage he turned on the donkey and killed him. The lion turned to the fox.

'If you will divide this food into two portions, we can each take our share and go home.'

The fox put the best, tenderest, choicest meats into one pile for the lion, taking only a few morsels for himself.

'Who taught you to divide up food like that?' asked the lion.

'Oh, I don't know. What happened to the donkey might have had something to do with it!' came the fox's reply.

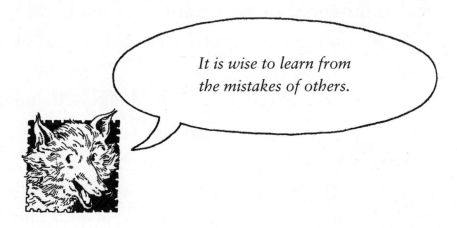

It is wise to learn from the mistakes of others.

The Goose Who laid Golden Eggs

A man once owned a goose who laid one gold egg each morning. But as time passed, the man grew more and more impatient with waiting for his special egg each day.

He said to himself, 'I bet that goose has got

a huge lump of gold inside.'

So he killed the goose and opened it up and surprise, surprise! There was no gold, just normal, ordinary goose innards.

If it's not broken, don't fix it! If something is working well, leave it alone.

The Fox and the Corn

A farmer caught the fox who had been stealing corn from his corn field and decided to have some fun. He tied some kindling to the fox's tail and set it alight. How he laughed as the poor fox ran around in agony. But

his laughter soon turned to anguish and tears as the fox, distraught with pain, ran up and down the farmer's corn field setting all his corn alight and destroying his crop for that year.

We should never give way to spite.

The Shipwreck

There was a terrible storm. A ship was being pummelled by the savage wind and huge waves and soon it began to sink. Everyone on board jumped off the ship and started swimming for their lives. All, that is, except one man. He stayed on board as the ship was going down, crying out, 'Save me.

Athena, save me and I will place gems and the finest foods and wines on your altar.'

From the sea below, another man called out to him, 'Don't leave it all to Athena. Let your arms and legs do some of the work as well!'

> *Don't leave your future solely to destiny or others. You have to put some effort in for yourself too.*

The Mouse and the Lion

A sleeping lion was wakened up by a mouse running over him. Catching the mouse with one paw, the lion was just about to snack on her when the mouse begged,

'Please don't eat me. I'm not even a morsel for a big lion like you. If you spare my life, I promise that some day, in some way, I will repay you.'

The lion thought about it and, admiring the mouse's courage, said, 'You're right. You aren't even a mouthful. You're barely worth me opening my mouth! So I'll let you go. But I don't see what a tiny thing like you could ever do to repay me, so you'll forgive me if I don't hold my breath!'

The lion let the mouse go nevertheless.

A few days later, the lion was caught in a huntsman's net and couldn't get out, no matter how hard he struggled. The mouse saw that the lion was trapped. Without a word, she chewed through first one section of rope, then another and another. Very soon, the lion was free.

'Thank you, friend mouse. I thought I was done for,' said the lion.

'I told you I'd be able to repay you one day,'

said the mouse. 'Aren't you glad now that you spared my life?'

Don't mock those smaller and more helpless than you. One day you may need their help. Kindness brings rewards.

The Fox and the Wild Boar

A fox was out for a walk one day when he came across a wild boar, sharpening his tusks against the trunk of a tree.

'Why on earth are you doing that?' asked the fox. 'There's nothing to fear here. There's no danger anywhere around us, no huntsmen in sight.'

'Which is why I'm doing it now,' said the boar.

'When there is danger around me, I won't have time to stop and sharpen my tusks.'

Be prepared.

The Frogs Want a King

'We want a king!'
'We should have a ruler!'
'We need a king!'
The frogs went to Zeus and asked him to give them a king. Fed up with their complaining, Zeus threw an old stick into their pond home.

'He's not much of a king.'
'He just lies around all day.'
'He never speaks and never moves.'

'What use is he?'

So the frogs went back to Zeus and complained about the king they'd been given. Furious at their attitude, Zeus threw a water snake into the frogs' pond and the water snake set about eating as many frogs as he could get his fangs into.

Be careful if you complain about someone in charge. You might end up with someone much worse to take their place.

The Bird and the Bat

A bird sat in her cage by a window. She waited silently for the sun to set and the sky to get dark before she started singing. A bat flying past the window asked

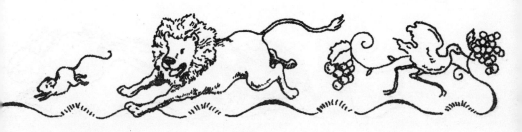

the bird, 'Why do you never sing until it gets dark?'

The bird replied, 'When I was free, I sang in the daytime and that's how I got caught. So it taught me a lesson and now I only sing at night.'

'Well, it's a bit late to take precautions now,' said the bat. 'You should've been more careful before you were caught.'

It's no good taking care after the damage has already been done. Be watchful before, not afterwards.

Mother Crab and Her Daughter

'Must you walk like that?' a crab mother complained to her daughter. 'Don't walk sideways.

158

It's so undignified, so common! Walk properly.'

'I certainly will, Mother,' said the daughter crab. 'Just as soon as you show me how it should be done.'

Example is the best teacher.

Snake Is Fed Up!

'Zeus! Zeus! I hate to complain, but I'm fed up!' said the snake.

'Fed up with what?' Zeus sighed.

'All day long people walk all over me,' the snake wailed. 'They trample on my tail, they march on my middle, they hop on my head.

That's why I'm fed up.'

Zeus replied, 'If you had bitten the first man who trod on you, the next one would've thought twice about doing the same thing.'

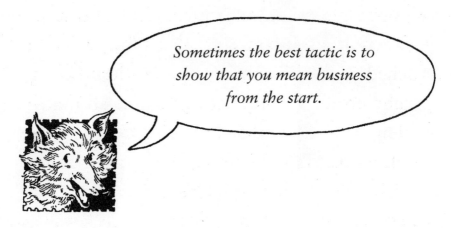

Sometimes the best tactic is to show that you mean business from the start.

The Stag's Mistake

As a stag stood drinking from a spring, he noticed his reflection in the water. 'Look at my gorgeous antlers!' he said to himself, turning his head this way and that. 'They are big and broad and quite stunning. But look at

my spindly legs. They're so knobbly and skinny, I can hardly bear the sight of them.'

Suddenly, from out of nowhere a lion appeared. The stag turned and ran for his life. On the open plain, he put a great deal of distance between himself and the lion. But when he reached wooded country, his antlers became caught up in the branches of a tree so that he couldn't run any further. In fact he couldn't move at all. As the lion was about to pounce, the stag thought bitterly, 'My legs which I scorned almost saved my life. And my antlers which I was so proud of have been the death of me.'

In bad times, we find out who is a true friend and who is the real enemy.

The Lark and Her Family

A lark made her nest in a field of corn so that her young would have plenty to eat until they were fully fledged and ready to fly. One day, the farmer came to the corn field and, seeing that his crop was ripe and dry, he said to himself, 'I'd better get my friends together to harvest my corn.'

One of the lark chicks heard him and told his mother.

'We don't have to go just yet,' said the lark.

The next day, the farmer came to inspect his corn and he said to himself, 'I shall get all my relatives to help me harvest my corn.'

The lark chick told his mother what the farmer had said.

'We still have a little time,' said the lark.

The next day, the farmer came to inspect his corn again, by which time the corn was so ripe the ears

of corn were dropping off in the heat of the sun.

'Right! That does it!' said the farmer. 'I'm going to hire some men and gather up the crop myself first thing tomorrow.'

When the lark chick told his mother what the farmer had said, the lark said, 'Now it is time to go. When a man relies on himself rather than on his family and friends, then things definitely get done.'

If you want to make sure something gets done, do it yourself.

The Rivers and the Sea

All the rivers got together and complained to the sea, 'When we reach you, our waters are fresh and clean and drinkable.

And then you turn us silty and salty.'

'If it upsets you,' said the sea, 'don't come!'

What cannot be cured, must be endured. What we can't change, we just have to put up with.

The Thirsty Crow

A crow was so thirsty she thought she would surely die from it if she didn't find water soon. She came across a large pitcher that had a small amount of water at the bottom. Try as she might, the crow's beak couldn't reach the bottom of the pitcher and the pitcher was far too heavy for her to tip over.

So the crow stood back and had a think. Then she had an idea. She picked up a pebble with her beak and dropped it into the pitcher. Then another and another. She kept at it until the water was at the top of the pitcher instead of the bottom and then she could drink.

Thinking first before rushing in will get the job done.

Mossycoat

Retold by Philip Pullman
Illustrated by Peter Bailey

There once was a widow who lived in a cottage, and she had a daughter. The girl was lovely, though she didn't know it, and nor did she know what her mother was making, for that was a secret she hadn't been told yet. It was a waistcoat kind of a thing, made of the greenest moss all sewn with gold thread that was finer than gossamer; and as for the stitches that held it together, no mortal ever stitched finer ones. A garment like that is a long time in

making, you can be sure; the widow was young when she started, and many years older by the time it was nearly finished.

For it wasn't done, quite, when the story begins.

One day a hawker came to the door. He was a nuisance, this old man. He wasn't content to sell his ribbons and laces and needles and pins, but he had to make familiar remarks and wink and pinch the cheeks of girls too gentle to say no. He hadn't been seen for a while; some said he'd been locked up for his wickedness; at any rate, he was out and about again, and when he knocked at the door, it was the daughter who opened it.

'Well, hello!' he said. 'You're a pretty one, ain't you?'

She didn't know how to answer that. *He* wasn't pretty by any means: he was snaggle-toothed and red-nosed, with lank hair combed over his greasy bald pate, and he strutted like a cocky little dog.

'Here,' he said, fumbling for her hand to pat it, 'you're the prettiest thing I seen since . . . ooh, ever. You're prettier than them roses round the door, dang me if you ain't. Here, look at this . . . '

He plucked off a rose petal and held it against her cheek, and he ran his knobbly old fingers over them both.

'I can't tell the difference!' he said. 'You're as soft and smooth as—'

But she shook her head like a wild thing, as shy as a fawn.

'Ooh, I like you,' he said. 'You got a spark in

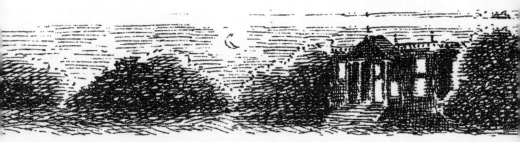

you. You got some fizz and crackle. Now I don't believe in beating about the bush: I'm looking for a wife, and I believe you'd make a good 'un. How about it? Eh? Eh?'

He was nudging and winking and licking his lips, and his rheumy old eyes were glistening. The girl said, 'Wait there.'

She shut the door and ran in to her mother.

'Mum!' she said. 'Mum! There's a horrible old hawker man at the door—'

'Oh, he's back, is he? What's he want?'

'He wants to marry me!'

'Well, do you want to marry him?'

'No, I don't!'

'All right,' said her mother, 'now you listen to me. You go and tell him that you'll marry him next week, as long as he brings you a dress. You understand? A white satin dress with gold sprigs on it, and it's got to fit you perfect.'

'And will I have to marry him then?'

'Go and do as you're told.'

So the girl went to the door and she said, 'Well, I don't know. But if I do marry you, I need a proper wedding dress. You come back next week with a white satin dress all covered in gold sprigs this big, no *this* big, and we'll see. Oh, and it's got to fit me perfect.'

'Hoo-hoo,' chortled the hawker. 'I'll be back! I'll be back! Giss a look at you, so I can judge your size.'

He held out his thumb and squinted one eye and measured her up and down, and off he went rubbing his hands.

Next week, there was a knock at the door, and

the girl looked out of the window and ducked her head back quickly.

'Mum!' she said. 'It's that blooming old hawker man, and he's got a parcel! What'm I going to do?'

'Go and answer the door, girl.'

So she opened the door slowly.

'Oooh,' said the hawker, 'what a little peach! Yum-yum-yum! Here's your dress, girl, just like you wanted. Now when are you going to—'

'Hold on,' said the girl, 'I said it had to fit me perfect. I got to try it on first.'

'Go on, then,' said the hawker, and he gave her the parcel. 'I'll wait here.'

She took the parcel in to her mother.

'Mum, he's brought me the dress!' she said. 'What am I going to do now?'

'Well, don't you want to try it on?'

They unwrapped the tissue paper and held up the dress. It was made of satin as white as snow, and the gold sprigs were all *this* big. And when she slipped it over her head and her mother fastened it up at the back, she found it fitted her like her own skin.

'Girl, you look beautiful,' said her mother.

'But I can't marry him, he's horrible!'

'Well, tell him you need another dress. Ask for a silk one this time, the colour of all the birds of the air.'

So she went back to the door. The hawker was twitching and sniffing with impatience.

'Well?' he said. 'Does it fit, then?'

'It's a bit tight under the arms,' she said, 'but I suppose it'll do to get married in. I can't go away

175

for the honeymoon in a wedding dress, though, I need another dress for that. Make it silk, the colour of all the birds of the air.'

'H'mm,' he said. 'And then . . . Mmm? Mmm? Eh?'

She just gave him a level kind of a look, and he made a whinnying sound and hurried away.

Next week, another knock.

'Mum, he's back again!'

'Open the door, then.'

The hawker thrust the parcel into her hands, and tried to snatch a kiss while he was about it. She moved her face out of the way and shut the door.

'He's getting impatient, Mum! I can't put him off for ever!'

'Never mind that. Try the dress on, girl.'

The silk dress fitted even better than the satin one had, and when she looked at herself in the mirror the girl felt dizzy to see the beautiful thing she was changing into. She wasn't sure if she liked it, but she knew she didn't like the hawker.

'What can I say to him?' she said in despair.

'Tell him you need some dancing shoes.'

So she said to the hawker, 'Well, I suppose the dresses are all right. But I expect there's to be dancing at the celebrations, and unless you want to dance with a bride in hob-nail boots, you better get me some of them gold patent-leather slippers with little heels and diamond buckles. And if they don't fit me perfect—'

'Right you are!' he said. 'And that's it, is it? Nothing else you want?'

'No,' she said, because she couldn't think of anything else.

'Giss a look at your feet then.'

He made a mark on a scrap of paper to get the size.

'Next week, then!'

'All right. 'Bye.'

Glumly she waited, and sure enough, next week there came his knock at the door.

'I got 'em! Diamond buckles and all! Now you got to marry me, girl, you can't keep me waiting any longer!'

'I got to try 'em on first,' she said. 'You probably made 'em too big. I got very little feet.'

'Oooh, I guarantee they'll fit,' he said, winking and rubbing his hands.

She tried them on, and she didn't need a shoe-horn: they were neat and soft and light, neither too small nor too big, and they twinkled like fireflies.

'Oh, Mum, what am I going to do now?' she wailed.

'Well now, girl,' said her mother, 'your mossy coat is all but ready. I should think another night's work'll see it done. So you go and tell the hawker to come back in the morning, about ten o'clock.'

'What mossy coat?' said the girl. 'What are you talking about?'

'Shoo! Go and tell him, go on!'

So the girl opened the door once more. The hawker was licking his lips and rubbing his hands and panting and shifting from foot to foot.

'Well? Well? Well? Well? Well?' he said.

'The slippers are all right,' she said. 'The left one's a bit loose round the heel, but I suppose they'll do. You come back at ten in the morning, and I'll marry you.'

'Ten in the morning? Why not now?'

'Because I got to wash my hair, of course,' she said. 'Ten o'clock, and don't be late.'

She shut the door before he could say another word. She could hear him snuffling and mumbling outside, but soon he gave up and left.

'Ten o'clock!' he called as he shut the garden gate. 'Hoo! Hoo! Hoo!'

'Mum—' the girl began, but her mother shook her head.

'Don't you say a word, because I'm going to be busy all night. Fetch that old suitcase off the top of the wardrobe and pack them dresses in it, and the slippers too, wrap 'em all in tissue paper, go on. Then bring me a cup of tea.'

All night long the woman sewed. She worked till three whole candles had burned down and the daylight had come again, and just as the cock was crowing she snapped off the last gold thread with her aching fingers.

She stretched and yawned and woke the girl.

'Now you better get up,' she said, 'because if you lie there snoring and steaming all morning you're going to find yourself a-married to that old hawker whether you want to be or not. Get out of bed and wash yourself and then come down to the parlour. And bring the suitcase.'

A few minutes later the girl, clean and wide awake and fearful, lugged the suitcase downstairs.

'What's that?' she said. 'Is that the mossy coat?'

Her mother held it up against her. It was as green as a spring morning, as fresh and soft as a breeze out of the west. All the mosses her mother had gathered from pond and meadow and

millstream over eighteen years were bright and living yet: she'd plaited and woven them so cunningly that all the tiny moss-leaves were still alive. And under and over and in between them all lay a shimmer of gold from those gossamer threads stitched with stitches too small to see. The mossy coat was so light and fine you could fold it all into a thimble, and yet so strong you couldn't tear it with your teeth.

And the best part was, it was magic. The daughter was to wear it under her other clothes when she wanted to make a wish, and whatever she wished for would come true.

'Oh, Mother,' the girl breathed, slipping her arms into it and hugging it close to her breast.

'Yes,' said her mother, 'this is for you, my dear. From now on, you're going to be called Mossy-coat. That's your name in the future. I been a-stitching and a-gathering since you were born, and now you're ready for it, and it's time for you

to leave and find your way in the world, my dear. You must go and seek your fortune, and a fine fortune it'll be. Take up the suitcase, and close your eyes, and wish you were a hundred miles away.'

'But what about him?'

'You leave him to me,' said her mother. 'Go on! Go!'

So Mossycoat took the suitcase in her right hand, and clenched her left hand firmly around the front of the mossy coat, and closed her eyes and wished. And as soon as the wish was formed in her mind, whoosh! Up she swept into the air, like a leaf in a storm, but she clung to the suitcase as tight as a limpet, and she clutched the mossy coat firm around her front.

Where she flew she couldn't tell, for she kept her eyes well shut; but presently all the whooshing died away, and then the soles of her feet touched ground and all her weight came back to

her, and she tottered a step or two and opened her eyes.

And there she was, in a different part of the country altogether. To her left was a river with green meadows beyond it, and to her right there were orchards and farmyards all neat and prosperous, and ahead of her was a hill, and on the top of the hill was a fine brick house with rose-beds in front and tulips standing to attention like soldiers along the gravel drive.

'Well,' said Mossycoat to herself, 'I can't stand here gaping all day.'

So first she took off her mossy coat and folded it away safe in the suitcase, and then she climbed

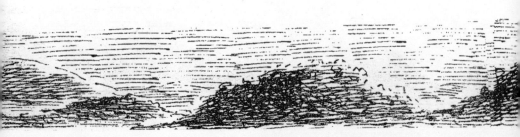

the hill in the warm sunshine with the birds singing and the breeze lifting the scent out of the apple-blossom, and she knocked on the door of the big house.

'Excuse me for knocking,' she said to the lady of the house, 'but I've just arrived in this land, and I need a job.'

The lady was a kind sort of a person, and shrewd, and she liked the look of this young girl with her suitcase; so she said, 'And what can you do, my dear? Can you sew, or polish, or what?'

'I can cook a bit,' said Mossycoat. 'There's some says I'm quite a good cook, or I will be with practice.'

'Well,' said the lady, 'if we needed a cook we'd try you out; but I tell you what,' she said, 'I'll give you a job in the kitchen and see how you get on.'

'Thank you, ma'am,' said Mossycoat, and she followed the lady into the house.

And such a house it was: a grand hall with a staircase all hung with paintings, and a drawing-room with gilded furniture and Chinese carpets, and a dining-room with a mahogany table so shiny that the silver candelabra seemed to be floating on dark water. The lady took Mossycoat up to a little bedroom in the attic and showed her where she could sleep and put her suitcase, and then took her down to the kitchen.

On the way through the hall there was a commotion, as a young man came in dressed for hunting, with half a dozen big floppy dogs all leaping up and licking him. Mossycoat took one glance at him, and then she kept her eyes modestly downwards and stood as meek as a nun.

'Who's this, Mother?' said the young man.

'She's our new kitchen maid,' said the lady. 'Come this way, my dear, and I'll show you where you'll be working.'

Mossycoat followed her into the kitchen. All

the cooks and the under-cooks and the bottle-washers and the pantry-maids and the scullery-maids stopped what they were doing and looked at Mossycoat, and she just kept quiet and looked down. The lady explained what Mossycoat's duties would be, and then she left the kitchen.

As soon as she'd gone, the servants started.

'Look at her! Lady Muck!'

'Who does she think she is?'

'Too grand for the likes of us – little snob!'

'Sucking up to madam! There's no sucking up in the kitchen – no airs and graces in here!'

The head cook said: 'What's your name, then?'

'Mossycoat,' she said.

'Mossycoat? Bossyboots, more like. You're one of the workers now. None of your high-and-mighty ways down here – we'll knock that out of you quick enough, see if we don't.'

They were a very low kind of people in that kitchen. They had just enough sense to know what was better than they were, and just enough energy to hate it.

So Mossycoat set to work, and they gave her the dirtiest jobs: cleaning the sooty grease off the spits, scrubbing the scullery floor, scraping the mud off the potatoes. And they never stopped calling her names and mocking her, although she just kept herself quiet and modest and gave them no reason to. And every so often, when her back was turned, some oaf would take the skimmer, all greasy from the soup, and knock her on the head with it; and she never once complained or tried to hit back. What with all the work and the harsh treatment, her clothes were soon

covered in grease and dirt, and her face and hair and fingernails were sadly grubby.

Now a little while later, it was announced that there were going to be three days of merry-making in a great house nearby. There was to be music, and dancing, and feasting, and fireworks, and invitations were sent out to all the houses in the district. Of course the master and mistress were invited, and the young master too, and it was the talk of the kitchen.

'I wish I could go – I'm as good as they are any day of the week!'

'All them lovely dresses . . .'

'All them handsome young men! Eh?'

Mossycoat said nothing. But all this time, the mistress of the house had been watching her, and she noticed what the servants didn't: she saw how clever and modest little Mossycoat was, and how pretty she was too, under the grime.

So she sent for her and said, 'Now, Mossycoat, how would you like a treat? How would you like to come to the ball with us, as our guest?'

'Well, ma'am,' said Mossycoat, 'that's very kind of you, but I think I'd better not, on account of being so grubby. I'd make your carriage all greasy if I sat in it. And I wouldn't know how to behave at a grand affair like that, and I'd let you down. Thank you kindly, but you'd be better off not taking me.'

'Well, are you sure?' said the lady, but Mossycoat wouldn't be budged.

When she went back to the kitchen, the servants were all agog to know why she'd been sent for.

'Did she give you notice?'

'Are they getting rid of you?'

'What did she say?'

Mossycoat said, 'The mistress asked me to the ball, and I said no.'

'You blooming liar!'

'Do you hear that?'

'She says they asked her to the ball! Ruddy nerve!'

And out came the skimmer, and poor Mossycoat's head rang.

The first night of the festivities was such a success that the lady of the house sent for Mossycoat again.

'Mossycoat, my dear, are you sure you

wouldn't like to come? I know you'd enjoy it! And the master would like you to join us, and the young master too. There's going to be fireworks tonight!'

'Thank you kindly, ma'am, but I think I'd better not,' said Mossycoat.

But that evening, when the servants were all sitting round idly in the kitchen smoking or playing cards or gossiping, Mossycoat went to her room. First she washed herself from head to foot, and cleaned all the soot and grime and dirt off her skin and out of her hair. Then she slipped the mossy coat on and went down to the kitchen. She went round from one servant to the next, touching each of them and wishing, and as she touched them they fell asleep, their great greasy heads lolling down on the table or back open-mouthed in their chairs.

When they were all fast asleep and snoring, she went up and put on her white satin dress with

the gold sprigs, and the golden slippers, and she wished herself at the festivities.

Up she flew, through the warm night air, and down she was set outside the ballroom. The band was playing a waltz, and the chandeliers were glowing, and the movement of the ladies and gentlemen on the dance floor was like swans on a lake.

Well, no sooner had Mossycoat arrived than the young master saw her. He didn't recognize her, but he said to his mother: 'Look at that girl in the white dress, Mother! Isn't she beautiful? Where does she come from, I wonder?'

'If you go and ask her to dance, you might find out,' his mother said.

So he came up to her and asked for the next dance. She looked him full in the eyes and said, 'Thank you, sir, but I'd rather not dance just yet.'

And she wouldn't dance with him, nor with anyone else, and he had to be content with that. Nor would she tell him her name, nor where she came from, and for all he begged to know, she just laughed and teased and said, 'That's my secret.'

The only comfort he had was that she wouldn't talk to anyone else either, though she was gracious and polite and so lovely to look at that all the young men in the place clustered round to flirt.

Finally the young master went to his mother and said, 'Mother, if I don't find out who she is I'll go mad with despair, but she won't tell me. Can you ask her for me?'

The lady sat down with Mossycoat on the

terrace, and they sipped their wine and chatted. But the lady got no more out of her than her son; all the strange girl would tell her was that she came from a place where they hit her on the head with a skimmer.

'What sort of a place is that?' said the lady in surprise.

'Oh, I shouldn't think I'll be there long,' was all Mossycoat said in reply.

Then came the last dance, and the young master tried once more. 'Please dance with me!' he said. 'I'm longing to dance, and there's no one else I want to dance with but you.'

'Well,' said Mossycoat, 'just this once, then.'

And she held out her hand, and he led her out to the dance floor. She was as light in his arms as a bird of the air, he'd never found dancing so easy and joyful; but it didn't last, for no sooner had they danced down to the end of the ballroom than she slipped out of his grasp

and away through the door.

'No! Wait! Come back!' he cried, and he ran out after her, but there was nothing there in the dark, nothing at all, only the warm breeze and the stars and his beating heart.

Mossycoat wished herself back at the house, and first she changed out of her satin dress and put on her dirty old clothes again, and then she went down to the kitchen and woke up the servants.

'Have we been asleep all this time?' said the pastrycook.

'Oh! You won't tell, will you, Mossycoat?' said the scullery-maid.

'If you keep us out of trouble, I'll let you have my old dress,' said the housekeeper.

'I won't say a word,' said Mossycoat, and nor did she.

Next day the talk was all of the beautiful girl who'd come out of nowhere and appeared at the ball. No one knew who she was, though all kinds of rumours sprang up: she was a princess from Russia; she was the daughter of a millionaire; she wasn't a mortal at all, she was a fairy. And everyone was buzzing to see whether she'd turn up for the last night of the festivities.

As for the young master, he was desperate.

'Father,' he said, 'if I don't find out who that girl is and where she goes to, I'll explode. I want you to have my best horse ready and waiting outside the door of the ballroom, so if she runs out again I can go after her.'

'All right, son,' said his father, 'I won't let you down.'

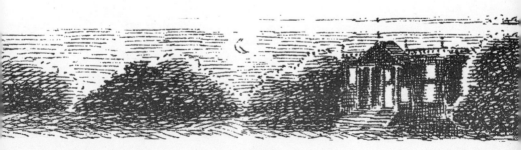

That evening Mossycoat put the servants to sleep
again, and this time she put on her silk dress the
colour of all the birds of the air. And when she
arrived at the ball this time, there was the young
master at once, at the head of all the other young
men desperate to dance with her; for word had
got around, and there wasn't anyone within fifty
miles who hadn't heard of this mysterious girl
who appeared out of nowhere and disappeared
again.

Mossycoat answered no questions except with
a smile, and she wouldn't dance with anyone –
except, once again, with the young master.

He was as proud and happy as a king; down

the ballroom they danced, and up again to the orchestra, and never had such a handsome couple been seen in anyone's memory. Then with a twirl in the music, the two of them turned and danced to the door –

And the young master must have loosened his grip in the heat of the moment, for she was out of his arms and away.

And straight he ran after her into the dark, and there was his horse with the groom at the reins –

'Oh, where did she go? Which way? Did you see her?'

No sign! Not a glimpse! She was vanished and gone. The horse shook his head and jingled his bridle, and stamped a hoof on the stones of the terrace; and the young master ran this way and that, gazing into the dark, calling, imploring the girl with no name to come back, for he loved her . . .

Nothing. Silence. Darkness.

The heartless music played on in the ballroom, and he heard none of it. Then as he turned in despair, he saw something catching the light, something down on the gravel below the windows, a little golden twinkle.

Her slipper! She'd dropped a slipper as she vanished! He clutched it to his heart. It was all that was left of that beautiful stranger, all that he had to take home from the ball.

Well, next day you never heard such a to-do.

It was the talk of every house in the county – the girl who'd won everyone's heart with her grace and her beauty, the young man she chose from all of the others to be her dancing-partner; and how she was nowhere to be found, and how he was lying ill in bed with a mysterious fever.

Mossycoat heard the rumours in the kitchen, with all the other servants.

'He's ill? The young master?'

'Groaning and sickening something terrible . . .'

'What's wrong with him?'

'They're in fear for his life!'

The doctor was sent for. He arrived in his carriage as soon as he could, and went straight up to the wild-eyed young patient. He tested his temperature and timed his pulse; he took his stethoscope out of his top hat and listened to the thumping of the young man's heart; he tapped his chest and peered into his eyes, and then he heard a broken whisper. The great physician stooped to listen closer, and then he saw what the young man clutched so tight in his hand.

He stood up straight and made his diagnosis.

'This is no fever,' he said solemnly. 'Nor is it an infection, nor a case of poisoning, nor a plague or a pox or a murrain. This is an affliction of the heart.'

'Oh no!' said the lady of the house, and she stroked the damp hair off her son's pallid brow.

'The patient is in love,' the doctor explained.

'That's the long and the short of it, and if he doesn't find the object of his affection, his heart will give way altogether. You must find the girl who fits this slipper' – and he held up the young man's trembling hand, still clutching the golden slipper – 'or else, send for the sexton to dig the patient's grave. My fee is ten guineas. Good morning.'

So that was the state of things. Word went out at once all over the countryside, and girls by the hundred came flocking to try the slipper, for it was announced that the young man was heir to a splendid fortune as well as being ardent and handsome. A line of girls led up the stairs, out through the hall, along the drive, and halfway

down the hill, and still more of them came from every direction.

And you never saw such feet: long knobbly ones, short fat ones, graceful ones but just too big, ones covered in corns and bunions, flat ones, warty ones, pretty ones and tender ones; but not a single one that fitted the slipper.

Eventually, when the last girl tugged her stocking up with a sigh and trudged off down the hill, the lady of the house said, 'We've tried everything else, my dear; we shall have to ask the servants.'

You can imagine the glee at that. Every female servant in the house crowded and jostled to shove her foot in the golden slipper, but of course none of them could do it, not even by holding their breath and squeezing.

The lady said, 'Is that everyone? I didn't see Mossycoat.'

'Oh, her,' said someone, but they had to fetch her.

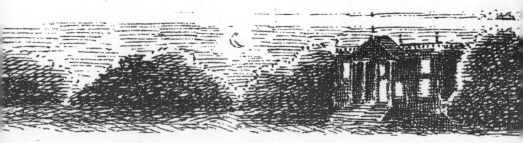

She came up the stairs all quiet and modest. Her hair was dusty, there was a smudge of soot on her cheek, and anything less like the girl of the night before would be hard to find; but the lady saw through her, and she felt a lift in her heart as Mossycoat slipped off her grimy shoe and took up the slipper.

And it fitted.

The young master gave a cry of joy, but Mossycoat held up her hand.

'No,' she said, 'wait. I'm not ready yet.'

She ran up to her bedroom and washed and put on the white satin dress, and the other slipper, and then came down to the young master's room, where all the family was waiting to welcome her. The young master ran to her and opened his arms, but again she said:

'Wait. I've changed my mind. I'm going to put my other dress on.'

So she went up and changed, and then she

came down once more, and this time she didn't say, 'Wait.'

Well, he nearly ate her.

And so they were married. There were celebrations and feasting and fireworks and fancy dress, and at the very height of the festivities, the lady said, 'Now tell me, Mossycoat dear, when we talked at the ball you told me you came from a place where they hit you on the head with a skimmer. Was that true?'

'Perfectly true,' said Mossycoat.

'And where was that place?'

'Well, it was in your kitchen,' said Mossycoat. 'And I said I didn't think I'd be there for long.'

'That was true enough,' said the lady, and kissed her.

And she sent for the servants and dismissed them all, the lazy cruel slubberdegullions, and set about hiring a better lot of servants altogether.

As for Mossycoat and her husband, they had a basket of children, and they're living there now in the house on the hill, as far as I know.

The Seal Hunter

Retold by Tony Mitton
Illustrated by Nick Maland

Here is a story handed down
from many a year ago.
The tale's been told by many
  a tongue
but I shall tell it so.

Duncan MacKinnon was a fisherman.
He sold his catch for a fee.
He lived in a lonely stone-built croft
by the side of the ragged sea.

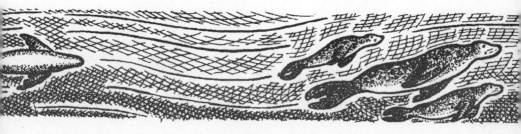

And when he could, he would hunt the seals
and strip them of their hides.
He would keep and cure each precious pelt
but throw each corpse to the tides.

Now in those days the pelts were prized
and folk would pay full well
for a sealskin cap, or a bag, or boots,
or clothes, as I've heard tell.

And the local folk came knocking
at the sealskin seller's door,
so in time he left his floats and nets
and hunted seals the more.

Duncan MacKinnon rowed the tides.
At his belt he wore a knife.
And with the aid of its deadly blade
he would take each sad seal's life.

The hunter soon grew stout and rich
with the sale of the skins he caught.
He lived his life by the skill of his knife,
but gave the seals small thought.

It was on a day, in a sunlit bay,
when the whole sea seemed to smile,
he sighted a huge and handsome seal
stretched out on a rocky isle.

When he saw the size of the great, grey seal
he crooned, 'With a skin like that
you could trim and shape a costly cape
or many a shoe and hat.'

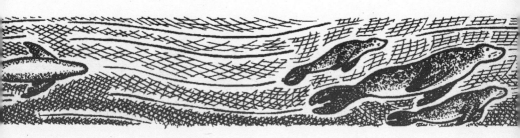

So he moored his boat but a short way off
and he crept up, yard by yard.
Then, almost there, he leaped through the air
and he drove his knife in hard.

But the great, grey seal was a fighter,
and he writhed from the hunter's grip.
With the knife in his side he dived for the tide
and he gave his man the slip.

MacKinnon shrugged and returned to his boat
to row to his own home shore.
'The seals in the sea swim wide and free,'
he mused. 'There are plenty more.'

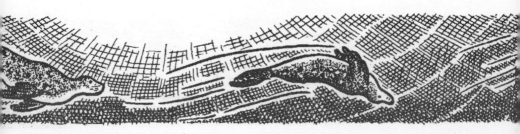

Duncan MacKinnon, oh, Duncan MacKinnon,
now take great heed, beware.
The fill of a purse can be a curse
for living things to bear.

The clink of a coin and its comfort
may keep you warm and dry.
But what of the shame that sticks to your name
at each sad creature's cry?

What is the worth of a wealth that's ripped
from the world by a ruthless knife?
What of the guilt on which it's built
as you strip each struggling life?

Duncan MacKinnon, when you were a boy,
did you never sit down on the beach
to learn from the pound of the stern sea-sound
the lessons that it might teach?

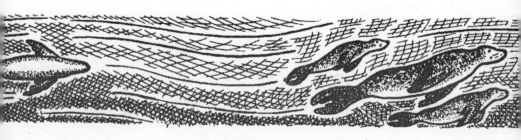

Faithless fisherman, when you were young,
did nobody think to tell
that there's more in the sea than a hunter's fee,
there's life in the great grey swell?

Did nobody show you, upon the shore,
when you were both young and small,
that the rolling sea, so fair and free,
is the Ancient Mother of All?

Sad seal hunter, learn in time,
as you stack your brimming store,
when simple need grows into greed
there'll be darkness at your door.

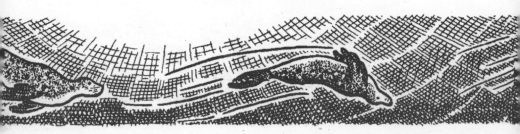

Late that night, as he sat by the light
of his guttering oil-lamp flame,
there came a knock at his low croft door
and a voice called out his name.

In a place so lone, at an hour so late,
who could this caller be?
The curious hunter loosed the door
and peered out cautiously.

There on the threshold stood a man
in a cape both dark and long.
He spoke to the wary hunter
in a deep voice, soft yet strong.

'Duncan MacKinnon, say, is it so,
you have seal skins here to sell?
Are you that famous hunter
of whom the folk all tell?'

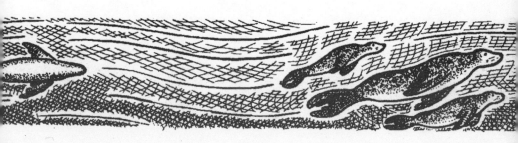

Duncan MacKinnon nodded.
'Of skins I have full store.
I'll sell you all the skins you need.
The sea holds plenty more.'

The dark-caped stranger listened
to the words the hunter told.
'My master waits nearby,' he said,
'if you wish your skins all sold.'

Duncan MacKinnon and the stranger
walked out to the edge of the land.
'Now where,' said the man, 'is my master?
He was here just now, at hand . . .'

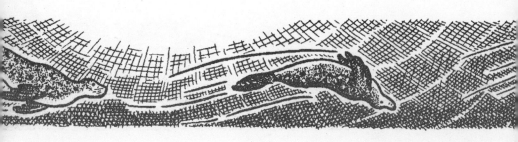

They peered at the edge of the clifftop
where the brink might break and slip.
It was then that the hunter felt his arms
held tight in a vice-like grip.

And before he could make a murmur
or shake his pinned arms free,
the stranger leaped from the clifftop
and they plummeted down to the sea.

As they hit the cold and dark of the waves
the stranger pulled him down.
The hunter felt his life was done,
for now he must surely drown.

Down they went, far deep beneath
the foam and the rolling waves,
till they came to an underwater world
where the rocks were pierced with caves.

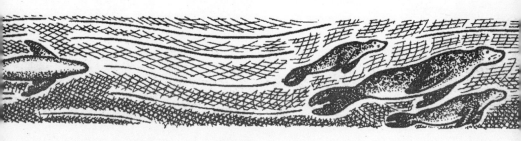

Still he felt the stranger's hands
where they gripped his arms so tight,
as together they swam through the mouth
  of a cave
and into a greeny light.

And down in that weird and greeny light
where he thought to meet his death,
when his will gave way and he drank the brine
he found he could draw his breath.

Now as he drank that liquid brine
he felt both light and free.
And the eerie glide of his sinister ride
seemed neither of land nor sea.

It was then that he noticed the skin of his guide
had a silky, a slippery feel.
In the watery light he saw to his fright
that the man had become a seal.

Gone were the hands and gone were the feet,
and gone was the long, black cape.
For now the dark guide that he floated beside
was wholly a seal in shape.

His silent seal-guide drew him on
to an underwater town
where the walls shone white with a pearly light
and the seals swam up and down.

They swam till they came to a palace
and they passed on through its door.
And once inside his eyes went wide
at the sight the hunter saw.

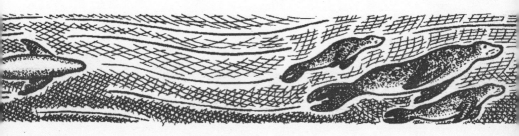

There were white rock seats in a circle
where many a seal sat round.
But in that solemn circus
there came not ever a sound.

For there in the circle's centre,
set out on a white rock bed,
lay a seal so still and silent
it seemed that seal lay dead.

Then the hunter saw the knife in its side
and he opened his mouth to moan.
There on its hilt was the ring of gilt
that marked it as his own.

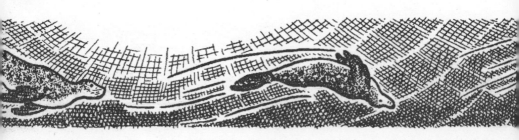

He fell to his knees on the chamber floor
and wrung his hands in fear.
Alone, deep down in the selkie town
he sensed his end was near.

But the seal-guide's voice spoke up to him
and seemed to fill his head.
'Remove the knife and smooth the wound,'
that strange voice softly said.

The hunter pulled his cruel knife out
and wiped its blade of steel.
When, with his hand, he smoothed the wound,
he saw it swiftly heal.

The great seal stirred and seemed to stretch,
then reared up proud and high.
He turned toward the hunter
and fixed him with his eye.

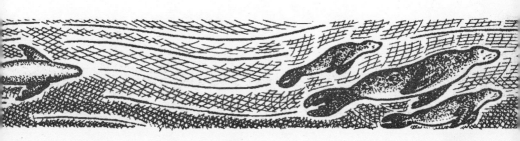

'I am the King of the Seals,' he said.
'Your seal-guide is my son.
The time has come to settle up
the deeds that you have done.

'Tonight my son has brought you here
to gather back your knife.
And if you now repent your deeds
I'll grant you back your life.

'If you will fish the seas again
and do the seals no ill,
we seals will always be your friends
and help your nets to fill.

'But if you slay a seal once more
and take it for its skin,
the Selkie Folk will seek you out
and slay you for your sin.

'Now stand again, and sheathe your knife
and say before us now,
will you give up the hunter's life
and take the Selkie Vow?'

The hunter rose and sheathed his knife,
then, there upon the sand,
he saw appear these words so clear,
as if by secret hand:

I, *who live by swell of sea,*
will learn to use it modestly,
to fish it but for honest need,
and not to grasp with rising greed.

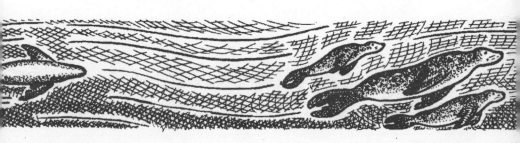

I, *who ride on wealth of wave,*
will vow to cherish, succour, save,
never to pluck or cruelly plunder
what goes over, on or under.

I, *who tell the turning tide,*
will make the sea my place, my pride,
and guard all things that go within,
whether of scale or shell or skin.

I, *who live beside the shore,*
will know content, not ask for more.
I am for her, and she for me.
The Selkie Vow respects the Sea.

The hunter stood and took the Vow
and at each word he spoke
the darkness seemed to gather round
and wrap him like a cloak.

He fell into a deep sea swoon
where waters rolled him round.
And when he woke it seemed to him
he lay on solid ground.

He raised his head and looked about.
The moon shone sweet and soft.
Above him on the cliff he saw
his stony fisher-croft.

He climbed the path and found his door,
then stumbled to his bed.
And all that night the strange events
went reeling through his head.

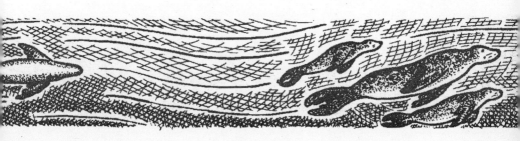

But when the light of early dawn
came trickling through his pane
he rose to fetch his fishing nets
and cast them once again.

And, from that time, if traders,
skin dealers, came to call,
he'd show them where his dagger hung,
sheathed safely on the wall.

He'd sit them at his table
and tell his story through,
of how he met the Selkie Folk,
and the king he nearly slew.

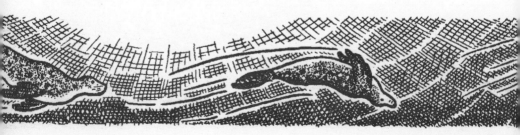

And how once more he fished the sea
and looked to it for life,
but never more would harm a seal
with net or club or knife.

And how, whenever he rode the waves,
in swollen tides or calm,
his nets were never empty
and he never came to harm.

My story's done and over,
my tale is at an end,
of how a cruel hunter
became the selkies' friend.

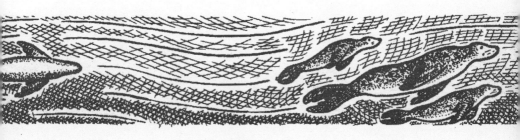

MAGIC BEANS

It is a story handed down
from many a year ago.
The tale's been told by many a tongue,
but I have told it so.

Grey Wolf, Prince Jack and the Firebird

Retold by Alan Garner
Illustrated by James Mayhew

O nce, long ago, not near, not far, not high, not low, at the place where seven rivers meet, there lived a king. And he was the king of the Stone Castle. He had three sons, and the name of the youngest was Prince Jack.

The king had a garden, too, and round it a wall. And in the garden there stood a tree. Gold was its trunk, and gold were its branches, gold its twigs, gold its leaves, and golden its fruit of

apples. And there was never a moment when the king of the Stone Castle did not keep guards about this wondrous tree.

One night, at deep midnight, there came a music into the garden.

It was music with wings,
Trampling things, tightened strings,
Warriors, heroes, ghosts on their feet,
Boguls and boggarts, bells and snow,
That set in sound lasting sleep
The whole great world
With the sweetness of the
calming tunes
That music did play.

The next morning, the king walked in his garden, and he saw that a golden apple had been taken from the tree.

'Who has stolen my apple of gold?' said the king of the Stone Castle.

'No one,' said the guard captain. 'We watched all night.'

'You did not,' said the king. And he made the guards prisoners, and sent them to work salt for ever.

'Now,' said the king, 'which of my beloved sons will watch my tree? I shall give half my kingdom now, and all of it when I die, to the son who will catch this thief.'

'I shall watch, Father,' said the oldest son. And that night he sat in the garden, his back against the tree.

At deep midnight, at dark midnight, there came a music over the wall.

It was music with wings,
Trampling things, tightened strings,
Warriors, heroes, ghosts on their feet,
Boguls and boggarts, bells and snow,
That set in sound lasting sleep
The whole great world
With the sweetness of the
calming tunes
That music did play.

And the oldest son slept.

The next morning, the king walked in his garden, and he saw that another golden apple had been taken from the tree.

'Who stole my apple of gold?' said the king of the Stone Castle. 'Who is the thief?'

'No one, Father,' said the oldest son. 'I watched all night.'

'Then tonight I shall watch,' said the second son. And the next night he sat in the garden, his back against the tree.

At deep midnight, at dark midnight, at blue midnight, there came a music into the garden.

It was music with wings,
Trampling things, tightened strings,
Warriors, heroes, ghosts on their feet,
Boguls and boggarts, bells and snow,
That set in sound lasting sleep
The whole great world
With the sweetness of the
calming tunes
That music did play.

235

And the second son slept.

The next morning, the king walked in his garden, and he saw that another apple had been taken from his tree.

'Who has stolen my golden apple?' said the king of the Stone Castle. 'Who is the thief?'

'No one, Father,' said the second son. 'I watched all night.'

'Then I shall watch,' said Prince Jack. And the next night he sat in the garden, his back against the tree. But he took his dagger and put it between his leg and the earth, the point upward, and the leg on the point.

At deep midnight, at dark midnight, at blue

midnight, at the midnight of all, a music came into the garden.

> *It was music with wings,*
> *Trampling things, tightened strings,*
> *Warriors, heroes, ghosts on their feet,*
> *Boguls and boggarts, bells and snow,*
> *That set in sound lasting sleep*
> *The whole great world*
> *With the sweetness of the*
> *calming tunes*
> *That music did play.*

And Prince Jack pushed his leg on the dagger, and a drop of his blood fell to the earth, but he did not sleep.

Then flew the Firebird, with eyes of crystal, over the wall, over the garden, to the tree.

And Prince Jack pushed his leg on the dagger, and a second drop of his blood fell to the

earth, but he did not sleep.

The Firebird perched on the lowest branch of the tree and took an apple in her beak.

Prince Jack pulled the dagger from his leg, and a third drop of his blood fell to the earth. He jumped to seize the Firebird, but his wound made him weak, and he caught hold of a tail-feather only, and the Firebird flew away.

Prince Jack wrapped the feather in his neck-cloth and sat down again beside the tree.

The next morning, the king walked in his garden, and he saw that another apple had been taken from the tree.

'Who has stolen the apple?' said the king of the

Stone Castle. 'Who is the thief?'

'It is the Firebird, Father,' said Prince Jack. 'I did not sleep. Here are three drops of my blood upon the earth. And here the feather for you to see.' And he unwrapped his neckcloth, and the garden, even in that morning, was filled with a flame of light.

The king of the Stone Castle said, 'It is the Firebird.' And he said to his two oldest sons, 'Go. I give you my blessing. Bring the Firebird to me; and what I promised before I shall give to the one who brings me that Bird.'

The sons took their father's blessing and rode away.

'Father, let me go too,' said Prince Jack.

'I cannot lose all my sons,' said the king. And Prince Jack went to his room and he thought; and he ran to the stables, took his horse, muffled its hooves and rode away.

He rode near and far, he rode high and low, by

lanes and ways and woods and swamps, for a long time or a short time; and he came to a wide field, a green meadow, an open plain. And on the meadow stood a pillar of stone, with words graven in it.

> *'Go straight, know cold and hunger.*
> *Go right, keep life, lose horse.*
> *Go left, keep horse, lose life.'*

'Dear horse,' said Prince Jack, and he turned to the right.

He rode one day. He rode two days. He rode three days. Then, in a dark forest, he met a Grey Wolf.

'Did you not read the rock?' said the Grey Wolf. And he took the horse, ripped it to bits, ate it; then went.

Prince Jack walked one day. He walked two days.

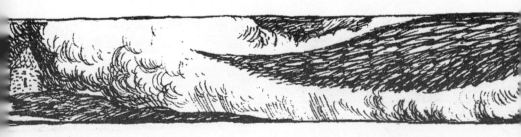

He walked three days. He walked until he was so tired that it could not be told in the story. And the Grey Wolf came to him again.

'You are brave enough,' said the Grey Wolf. 'So I shall help you. I have eaten your good horse, and I shall serve you a service as payment. Sit you up on me and say where I must take you. The roads are open to the wise, and they are not closed to the foolish.'

So Prince Jack sat up on the Grey Wolf.

The Grey Wolf struck the damp earth and ran, higher than the trees, lower than the clouds, and each leap measured a mile; from his feet stones flew, springs sprouted, lakes surged and mixed

with yellow sand and forests bent to the ground. Prince Jack shouted a shout, whistled a whistle, snake and adder hissed, nightingales sang and beasts on chains began to roar. And the Grey Wolf stopped at a wall.

'Now, Prince Jack,' he said, 'get down from me, the Grey Wolf, climb over the wall, into the garden. It is the garden of the king of the Copper Castle. In the garden stand three cages. In the first cage there is a crow. In the next cage there is a jackdaw. In the golden cage there is the Firebird. Take the Firebird, put her in your neckcloth and come back. But do not, do not, do not ever take the golden cage.'

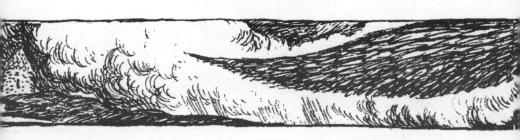

Prince Jack climbed the wall, passed the first cage, passed the second cage and put the Firebird in his neckcloth. But the golden cage was so beautiful. He picked it up, and there sounded throughout the garden and throughout the kingdom a great clang of bells and a twang of harps, and five hundred watchmen came and took him to the king of the Copper Castle.

'Why do you steal the Firebird?' said the king.

'The Firebird stole my father's golden apples,' said Prince Jack. 'And he is a king.'

'If you had come to me first, I should have given you the Firebird with honour,' said the king of the Copper Castle. 'But you came as a thief. How will it be with you now when I send through all kingdoms that your father's son brought shame within my borders?'

'The shame is great,' said Prince Jack. 'There is no place of honour left for me.'

'Then I shall give you one chance, since you

243

have been honest with me,' said the king. 'If you will ride across thrice nine lands, beyond the Tenth Kingdom, and get for me the Horse of the Golden Mane, I shall give you back your honour and, with all joy, the Firebird, too.'

The five hundred watchmen took Prince Jack to the bounds of the garden, and threw him out. The Grey Wolf came to him.

'You did not, and you would not, as I told you,' said the Grey Wolf. 'But this is not trouble yet. The trouble is to come. I have only a trotter and a sheep's cheek, and they must do.'

Prince Jack and the Grey Wolf ate the trotter and the sheep's cheek. Then Prince Jack sat up on the

Grey Wolf, and the Grey Wolf struck the damp earth and ran, higher than the trees, lower than the clouds, and each leap measured a mile; from his feet stones flew, springs sprouted, lakes surged and mixed with yellow sand and forests bent to the ground. Prince Jack shouted a shout, whistled a whistle, snake and adder hissed, nightingales sang and beasts on chains began to roar.

The Grey Wolf stopped at a white-walled stables.

'Get down from me, the Grey Wolf,' he said, 'into the white-walled stables. They are the white-walled stables of the king of the Iron Castle. Take the Horse of the Golden Mane. But do not, do not, do not ever take the gold bridle.'

Prince Jack went into the white-walled stables and took the Horse of the Golden Mane. But the gold bridle was too beautiful to leave. He picked it up, and a thunder sounded through the stables and five hundred grooms came and brought him

to the king of the Iron Castle.

'Why did you steal the Horse of the Golden Mane?' said the king.

'Because the Firebird stole my father's golden apples,' said Prince Jack. 'And he is a king. Then I stole the Firebird, but was caught as I am now.'

'If you had come to me first, I should have given you the Horse of the Golden Mane with honour,' said the king of the Iron Castle. 'But you came as a thief. How will it be with you now when I send through all kingdoms that your father's son brought shame within my borders?'

'The shame is great,' said Prince Jack. 'There is no place of honour left for me.'

'Then I shall give you one chance, since you have been honest with me,' said the king. 'If you will ride across thrice nine lands, beyond the Tenth Kingdom, and get for me the Princess Helen the Fair, whose skin is so clear that you see the marrow flow from bone to bone, I shall give

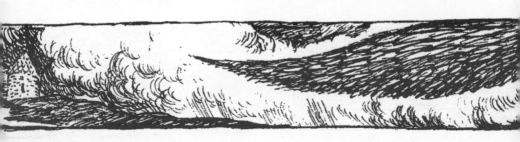

you back your honour and, with all joy, the Horse of the Golden Mane.'

The five hundred grooms took Prince Jack to the door of the white-walled stables and threw him out. The Grey Wolf came to him.

'You did not, and you would not, as I told you,' said the Grey Wolf. 'But this is not trouble yet. The trouble is to come. I have only a trotter and a sheep's cheek, and they must do.'

Prince Jack and the Grey Wolf ate the trotter and the sheep's cheek. Then Prince Jack sat up on the Grey Wolf, and the Grey Wolf struck the damp earth and ran, higher than the trees, lower than the clouds, and each leap measured a mile; from

his feet stones flew, springs sprouted, lakes surged and mixed with yellow sand and forests bent to the ground. Prince Jack shouted a shout, whistled a whistle, snake and adder hissed, nightingales sang and beasts on chains began to roar.

The Grey Wolf stopped at the golden fence of the garden of Princess Helen the Fair, whose marrow flowed from bone to bone.

'Get down from me, the Grey Wolf,' he said. 'Go back along the road by which we came, and wait for me in the field with a green oak tree.' So Prince Jack did.

But the Grey Wolf, he stayed.

And, at evening, the Princess Helen the Fair came into the garden, and her marrow flowed from bone to bone. The Grey Wolf jumped into the garden, seized her and ran off. He ran to the field of the green oak, where Prince Jack waited. Princess Helen the Fair dried her eyes fast when she saw Prince Jack.

'Sit up on me,' said the Grey Wolf, 'and hold the princess in your arms.'

Prince Jack sat up on the Grey Wolf, and held Princess Helen the Fair in his arms, and the Grey Wolf ran as only a wolf runs in story, until they came to the white-walled stables of the king of the Iron Castle with the Horse of the Golden Mane. But by now Prince Jack loved Princess Helen the Fair, and she loved him, and the Grey Wolf saw.

'I have served you in much,' said the Grey Wolf. 'I shall serve you in this. I shall be Princess Helen the Fair, and you will take me to the king, and he will give you the Horse of the Golden Mane. Then mount you the horse and ride far. And when you think of me, the Grey Wolf, I shall come to you.'

And the Grey Wolf struck the damp earth, and became a False Princess, and Prince Jack took him into the white-walled stables, while Princess

Helen the Fair stayed outside.

When he saw the False Princess, the king of the Iron Castle was pleased, and he gave Prince Jack the Horse of the Golden Mane with joy, and the gold bridle, and gave him back his honour, too. Then Prince Jack rode out of the white-walled stables on the Horse of the Golden Mane and put Princess Helen the Fair before him, and rode away.

The False Princess, the Grey Wolf, stayed one day in the king's palace. He stayed two days. And he stayed three. Then he asked the king if he might walk in the garden. So the king ordered serving-women to walk with the False Princess. And, as they walked, Prince Jack, far away, riding,

called, 'Grey Wolf! Grey Wolf! I am thinking of you now!'

The False Princess, walking in the garden with the serving-women, sprang up as the Grey Wolf, over the garden wall and ran as only wolves do in story until he came to Prince Jack.

'Sit up on me, the Grey Wolf,' he said, 'and let Princess Helen the Fair ride the Horse of the Golden Mane.'

And so they went on together.

At last, after a long time or a short time, they came to the palace of the king of the Copper Castle who kept the Firebird.

'Dear friend! Grey Wolf!' said Prince Jack. 'You have served me many services. Serve me one more.'

'I shall serve you once more,' said the Grey Wolf. And he struck the damp earth and became a False Horse, and Prince Jack mounted him and rode into the palace.

When the king of the Copper Castle saw the False Horse, he was pleased, and he gave Prince Jack the Firebird in its golden cage, and gave him back his honour, too.

Prince Jack left the palace and went to where Princess Helen the Fair was waiting with the Horse of the Golden Mane, and they rode towards the palace of Prince Jack's father, the king of the Stone Castle. They came into a dark forest.

And Prince Jack remembered, and called, 'Grey Wolf! Grey Wolf! I am thinking of you now!' And straight away the Grey Wolf appeared. But he said, 'Well, Prince Jack, here is where we met. I, the Grey Wolf, have paid for your horse. I am no more your servant.' And he jumped into a thicket and was gone.

Prince Jack wept, and rode the Horse of the Golden Mane, with the gold bridle, Princess Helen the Fair before him, and in her arms the Firebird and its golden cage.

They rode one day. They rode two days. They rode three days. But whether the way was long or short, they grew tired, and when they came to the graven stone in the green meadow, they rested against it, and slept.

And as they slept, the two older brothers came back from their empty wanderings, and when they saw Prince Jack with the Firebird in its golden cage, and the Horse of the Golden Mane and its gold bridle, and Princess Helen the Fair, whose marrow flowed from bone to bone, they cut Prince Jack into four pieces, and threw the four pieces to the four winds, and took the Firebird and the Horse of the Golden Mane and Princess Helen the Fair with them

back to their father's palace.

The king of the Stone Castle was glad to see his sons and to hold the Firebird in its golden cage. And the two brothers drew lots, and the first won Princess Helen the Fair, and the second took the Horse of the Golden Mane, and a wedding was ordered.

But Prince Jack lay dead, by lanes and ways and woods and swamps, out on the green meadow, cut into four parts.

He lay one day. He lay two days. He lay three days. And, in the forest, the Grey Wolf smelled the flesh, and knew that it was the flesh of Prince Jack. He went to where the pieces lay. And there came a crow with brazen beak and brazen claws,

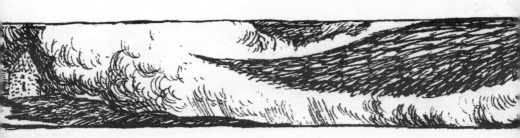

with her two children, to feed on the flesh. But the Grey Wolf jumped and seized one of her children.

'Grey Wolf, wolf's son,' said the crow, 'do not eat my child. Do not tear off its rash little head. Do not take it from the bright world.'

'Black Crow, crow's daughter,' said the Grey Wolf, 'serve me a service, and I shall not hurt your child. Fly for me over the Glass Mountains to the Well of the Water of Death and the Well of the Water of Life. Bring me back those waters, and I, Grey Wolf, shall loose your child. But, if not, I shall tear off its rash little head. I shall take it from the bright world.'

'I shall do you this service,' said the crow. And she flew beyond the end of the earth, over the Glass Mountains, and she came back with the Water of Death and the Water of Life.

The Grey Wolf tore the crow's child to bits. He sprinkled over it the Water of Death, and the bits

grew together. He sprinkled over it the Water of Life, and the crow's child awoke, shook itself, and flew away.

The Grey Wolf sprinkled the pieces of the body of Prince Jack with the Water of Death. And the pieces were joined. He sprinkled the Water of Life. And Prince Jack stretched himself, yawned, and said, 'How long have I been asleep?'

'Yes, Prince Jack, and you would have slept for ever, had it not been for me, the Grey Wolf. Long hair, short wit. Sit up on me, for your oldest brother is to wed Princess Helen the Fair this very day.'

Prince Jack sat up on the Grey Wolf, and the Grey Wolf struck the damp earth and ran, higher than the trees, lower than the clouds, and each leap measured a mile; from his feet stones flew, springs sprouted, lakes surged and mixed with yellow sand and forests bent to the ground. Prince Jack shouted a shout, whistled a whistle, snake and adder hissed, nightingales sang, beasts

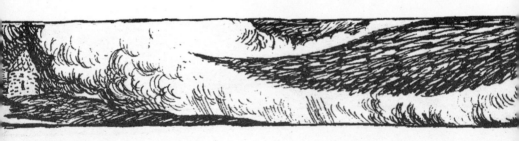

on chains began to roar, all the way to the palace
of the king of the Stone Castle.

Prince Jack got down from the Grey Wolf in the
middle of the wedding, and when she saw him
alive, Princess Helen the Fair ran to him, and they
told the king all that had happened.

The anger of the king was a river in storm, and
he called a halt to the wedding, made his oldest
son a scullion, his second son a cowherd and fed
them all their days on cockroach milk. But Prince
Jack and Princess Helen the Fair were married
that same night. And on all sides those that weep
were weeping, those that shout were shouting
and those that sing were singing.

Prince Jack said, 'Grey Wolf! Grey Wolf! How can I repay you? Stay with me for ever. You shall never want. Go now for ever through my ground. No arrow will be let at you. No trap will be set for you. Take any beast to take with you. Go now through my ground for ever.'

'Keep your herds and your flocks to yourself,' said the Grey Wolf. 'There is many a one who had trotters and sheep as well as you. I, the Grey Wolf, shall get flesh without putting trouble here. The tale is spent. Live long, Prince Jack. Live happy. But me you shall see never more.' And the Grey Wolf struck the damp earth and was gone.

Prince Jack and Princess Helen the Fair lived in friendship and they lived in peace, they lived happily and they lived long; and if they are not dead yet, they are living still, and they feed the hens with stars.

But the Grey Wolf they did not see; though you may. And, if you do, what then?

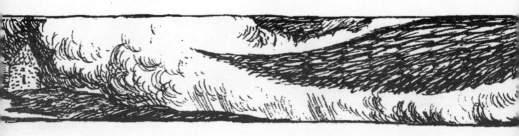

The Snow Queen

Retold by Berlie Doherty

Illustrated by Siân Bailey

Long ago in the cold north there were some wicked imps. Just for something to do they made a mirror. It wasn't like any other mirror. It made roses look like cabbages and birds look like flying toads. It took the beauty out of everything, and if the object had an ugly heart, the mirror found it and reflected it. The imps had great fun with that mirror.

They dared each other to show it to the most beautiful creature on the earth, the Snow Queen.

'Go on, you do it,' they cackled to each other. 'Let's see how deep her famous beauty really is.'

Well, the Snow Queen loved mirrors. She tossed back her long white hair and smiled, but all she saw in her reflection was her black and evil heart.

'How dare you show me this!' she screamed.

She was so angry that she struck her fist into the mirror and broke it into a thousand pieces, which shattered into the night sky and looked, for a moment, like stars. But then the sparkles of dust floated through the air and some of them landed in people's hearts just as if they were splinters of glass, and turned them to ice. The wicked imps screeched with laughter.

'Look, look what our mirror's done! There'll be some precious mischief now! It's better than ever!' And they scurried into their slimy holes and waited to see what would happen next.

Well, it happened to a boy and girl called Kay and Gerda. They lived in the top rooms of very tall houses that faced each other, in the town of Amsterdam. They didn't have gardens, but they each had window-boxes where they grew their flowers. There was a bridge from Kay's window to Gerda's, so they could walk across to each other's rooms high above the streets. And on the bridge there grew a rose tree that belonged to them both. In summer they used to watch the flowers opening out.

> 'We count the petals on our tree
> A rose for you, a rose for me.'

That was their song.

And in the winter, when it was too cold to play out and the frost made feathery patterns on the windows, Gerda would warm a coin and hold it against the glass to melt the ice. Then she would look through the spy-hole and see Kay looking at her from his window. He would run down his stairs and climb up to Gerda's room, and together they would listen to the tales her grandmother told, all about the animals she used to talk to. The snow would be flurrying against the window like a flock of white butterflies, and one day Grandmother told them to watch out for the Snow Queen, who had a wicked heart.

'If she ever came in here I'd put her on the stove and melt her!' Kay said.

That night in bed, Kay saw the Snow Queen. He opened his eyes and there she was, all in a shimmer of silvery light, peering at him through his frosty window and laughing down at him –

but when he reached out to the glass she disappeared, as if the touch of his warm hand had melted her away. Or maybe he had only dreamed he saw her. That could be it.

But he should not have forgotten about her. Summer came again. Grandmother brought them both presents from the market – a pair of red shoes for Gerda, and a pair of boots for Kay. They wore them at once, even though Kay's were a bit big for him and creaked when he walked. 'I like them like this,' he said.

'You sound like a squeaky mouse!' laughed Gerda. 'And aren't my shoes beautiful! They're my treasure!'

They walked backwards and forwards across their flower bridge, and suddenly a wild wind whipped around them, glittering with silver dust. They clung to each other. Some of the dust went in Kay's eye and drifted down to his heart. It stabbed him there as if it were a blade of ice, and he gasped out loud with pain. He thought he was going to die.

'Kay! What's the matter?' Gerda asked, but he pushed her away roughly.

'Leave me alone. I hate you,' he said.

She stared at him, not understanding what had come over him.

'Go away!' he shouted.

Gerda didn't know that he had splinters of glass in his heart, and that it had already turned to ice. How could she know? 'Can't I help you?'

'Go away. I can't bear to look at you,' he said. 'You're so ugly.'

He tore down the rose tree that they loved so

much. 'Pooh, it stinks!' he said, and threw it over the bridge into the street below, where the carriages trundled across it and mashed it into the ground. And then he ran into his house, shouting to her that he never wanted to play her silly games again. 'And I hate these stupid squeaky boots!'

'I don't know what's happened to Kay,' Gerda sobbed, and the grandmother put her arms round her and comforted her. She thought in her heart that she knew what had happened, but she said nothing. What could be done?

Before long, summer turned to winter and petals of snow came drifting down from the sky. Gerda

pressed a hot penny to her window and made a hole in the ice. Imagine how happy she was to see Kay looking at her from his window across the bridge.

'Kay! Will you come and play now?' she laughed, but he shouted back, 'Don't be stupid. I'm looking at the snow crystals. Anyway, I'm going to play out with the big boys.'

He stomped down all the noisy stairs of his house with his old sledge across his shoulder, and went to the far field at the end of town where all the older boys were playing. They laughed when they saw him, because everyone knew how sour and grumpy he was; not much fun in him at all. They were pulling each other about on their sledges, but nobody wanted to pull Kay along.

Then into all the clamour and laughter there came the sound of galloping hooves, and the whoosh of a sleigh that was rushing across the ice. A team of white horses with flickering manes

was pulling a sleigh that glittered like diamonds. Driving it was a woman dressed all in white, looking neither to the right of her nor to the left of her. She reigned in the horses and came to a stop, and everybody could see how beautiful she was.

'How about hitching a ride on that!' said one of the boys, and the others all whistled and shook their heads. Nobody dared, it was so grand. Besides, it was so fast.

But Kay ran across to it. 'I will!' he shouted. 'Just watch me.'

Well, the boys didn't believe for a second that he'd do it, but he did. He tied his sledge to the back of the silver sleigh. As soon as he clambered

back on to it again the beautiful woman laughed, and Kay knew at once that he had heard that laugh before. The woman cracked her whip and away sped the horses, and the sleigh behind it, and behind that came Kay, bumping along on his old wooden sledge – and behind him, all the boys of Amsterdam, until they stopped, gasping for breath.

Kay clung on to his rope for dear life. 'Stop! Stop!' he shouted, as he was flung from side to side of his sledge. 'Please stop!' Bit by bit his battered sledge dropped to pieces, so he was being dragged on his stomach along the ice. 'Stop!' he screamed, and, at last, she did.

'Climb up into my sleigh, child.' She wrapped a warm fur cloak round him. 'Now, Kay. Don't you know me?'

And he did know her, of course. 'You're the Snow Queen, aren't you?'

She put her arm round him and kissed him.

'You're safe with me,' she said.

She pulled at the reigns and once again the sleigh started forward, but this time it rose up into the night sky, among the stars and the moon. Sometimes Kay slept and sometimes he was awake, with the wind cold on his face. They flew across land and they flew across sea, they flew across white mountains to the far, far north of the world where nothing moved. Everything they could see was frozen into solid ice. The Snow Queen whipped her horses again and down and down they galloped, until they came to a palace that was made of blue ice.

Deep inside the palace was a great hall that glittered and rang with the tinkle of icicles. The Snow Queen said, 'This is my home, and it is your home, Kay. For ever.'

Kay loved her so much that all he wanted to do was to stay with her. He forgot about his home and his family. He forgot all about Gerda.

People said that Kay would never come home again. They watched out for him until the end of winter, and then they gave up watching. They said that he was dead. When Gerda heard them saying this she knew she must try to find him. She kissed her sleeping grandmother goodbye and ran out of the house, down to the river and along its banks until she was out of sight of the town. She was sure that the river had swallowed him up, and that the river could bring him back. She took off her new shoes and threw them into the water, saying, 'River, I'll give you my new red shoes if you'll only tell me where Kay is.' Whether the river knew or not, it wouldn't say, but would only laugh.

Gerda knew she must carry on searching. She slept in a garden of flowers and when she woke up and saw the roses she thought of Kay and knew she must carry on searching. She heard the birds over her head singing, and asked them if they knew where Kay was, but whether they did or not, they wouldn't say.

So Gerda walked on into the cold of the forest, and there she met with a crow who asked her where she thought she was going in her bare feet.

'I'm looking for my best friend, Kay,' she told him. 'People say he's dead but I know he can't be. Can you help me to find him?'

The kind-hearted crow wanted so much to help her that he flew to a castle to ask his sweetheart, and she sent him back with a message to say yes, a boy just like Kay had turned up that very day and married the princess.

'Life's full of little surprises, isn't it!' the pleased crow said.

Gerda ran through the forest and tiptoed through the castle to the very room where the new prince lay sleeping. She saw his golden hair and 'Kay!' she called to him, but when the boy sat up she saw that it wasn't Kay at all. And there was the princess, demanding to know what Gerda was doing in her castle with no shoes on her feet.

'I'm looking for my best friend, Kay,' Gerda told her. 'People say he's dead but I know he can't be.'

'Poor you,' said the princess. 'But you can't go on like this.'

She gave Gerda warm clothes to wear, and strong boots to put on her feet, and a golden carriage lined with biscuits and peppermints to ride in. She kissed her goodbye and she and the young prince with the golden hair, the crow and his sweetheart all wished her luck in her search for Kay.

Deep in the blue heart of the palace Kay spent his days moving blocks of ice across the frozen floor, just to entertain the Snow Queen.

'Can I go out?' he asked her, weary of his task. He wanted to ride away with her when she went on her journeys.

'Where to? What for?' she laughed, and her laughter was like the shattering of glass. She stroked his hair. 'One day you shall have the freedom of the world!'

'Will I have a new sledge?'

'Yes, that too!' she called, as she rose away from the palace in her gleaming sleigh. 'But first you must find me the secret of the universe,

or you will never be free.'

And so Kay toiled on, trying to make patterns with his ice blocks to solve the great mystery. And he was all alone in the great hall, and had forgotten how to laugh or how to sing.

Gerda hadn't travelled more than a night and a day when her coach was raided by a band of robbers. They killed the coachman and would have killed Gerda too, if the Robber Queen's daughter hadn't said she wanted her for a playmate. She stole her boots and muff and then bundled Gerda into the hall of the robbers, which was flickering with candlelight and reeking with the smells of robbers and animals. The bearded Robber Queen sang lustily and did cartwheels along the great long table, putting her great fists in all the plates of food, but the Robber Girl wouldn't let Gerda stay and watch. She pulled her into her room to look at her pigeons and her pet reindeer.

'His name's Baa-baa,' said the Robber Girl. 'Go on, give him a kiss!'

But to her great surprise Gerda cried because the animals weren't free. 'You're an odd one!' the Robber Girl said. 'But you'll have to be my friend or Ma will have you for supper.'

'Would she really?'

'Snip snip snee! I'll say she would! Couldn't you see her sparking her greedy little eyes at you?'

The Robber Girl slept with a dagger under her straw mattress in case Gerda tried to escape. But during the night something amazing happened. Gerda heard the pigeons talking together.

'We know where Kay is!' they cooed. 'We do! We do! He's with the Snow Queen.'

'The Snow Queen!' said Gerda, remembering Grandmother's stories. 'But where does she live?'

And the reindeer sighed and said, 'Ah! The Snow Queen! She lives in Lapland, where I come from. If only I were free to wander in the

snowy mountains again!'

Gerda woke the Robber Girl and begged her to let the reindeer take her to Lapland.

'Reindeers can't talk,' said the Robber Girl crossly. 'And besides, he's my pet. And anyway, I want you to stay here to be my friend.'

'Then you'll know how I feel,' Gerda said. 'I want to find my friend, Kay. People say he's dead but I know he can't be. Please help me.'

The Robber Girl stared at Gerda, and knew she would have to let her go. She helped her to sneak out of the robber hall and put her on Baa-baa's back. 'Goodbye, sloppy chops,' she said to him. 'Look after my friend.'

They galloped through dark forests and climbed up into the white-headed mountains, and around them wolves howled and ravens croaked. At last they came to Lapland, and by this time Gerda was almost frozen stiff with cold. Baa-baa hammered with his antlers on the door of a tiny house until an old woman opened it up. She had eyes as flat as fishes and layers of clothing like birch bark hanging on her skin.

'Oh, it's you is it?' she said. 'What do you want?'

Gerda was so cold that she could hardly speak. 'I'm looking for my friend. The Snow Queen has taken him.'

'Well, she's gone to Finmark,' the old woman said. 'Now don't bother me with your tears. You'd better come in and warm yourselves with a bowl of fish stew.'

While Gerda and Baa-baa were eating, the Lap woman wrote a message on a piece of dried fish

and told them to take it to her friend the Finn woman. So Gerda climbed on to the reindeer again and on they went. Baa-baa's hooves chimed on the frozen earth. Nothing moved around them; no streams, no birds. And they came to Finmark.

'How can anything live here?' Gerda asked. They found a house that was buried so deep in the snow that all they could see was blue smoke coming from a hole. Gerda had to climb down through the chimney, and the reindeer followed her, protesting loudly that he'd rather stay outside and freeze than go indoors and sweat to death.

'Get me out of here!' he bellowed. 'I'm going to faint.'

There inside the smoky darkness of her den was the oldest woman Gerda had ever seen, with hardly a stitch of clothing on because it was so hot inside her house of snow. It was almost as if she was expecting Gerda. She held out her hand for the piece of fish and read the message, nodding and muttering. Then she put the fish into a stew that was bubbling on the fire, and sank into such a deep silence that Gerda thought she had fallen asleep and forgotten about her.

'Please will you help me?' she whispered, trying not to cry.

'Yes, wake up and help her,' said the reindeer, scratching the old woman with his antlers. 'Her best friend Kay has disappeared, and everyone says he's dead, but she knows he isn't.'

'I know all that,' said the old woman. 'Don't hurry me.' And she closed her eyes again.

'You know everything,' the reindeer went on,

'but all you can do is sleep. Can't you tell Gerda what she must do?'

The old woman didn't even bother to open her eyes. 'No one can help her.' She mumbled as if she was in a dream, although in fact she was thinking so deeply that she had travelled round the world and back in her head. 'She's managed to come all this way in her bare feet, all for the love of a friend. What more could anybody do?' And then she dropped her voice still lower, so Gerda couldn't hear her over the crackling of the fire, and the reindeer only caught the words because his ears were so big. 'She has such goodness. She has it in her heart to find Kay, and she will.'

Then she opened her eyes and stared at Gerda. 'Are you brave enough to go into the Snow Queen's palace on your own?'

'Yes,' said Gerda, though she couldn't help trembling.

'It's only ten miles from here. Have some fish, and off you go.'

The reindeer left Gerda in the garden of the Ice Palace, and said goodbye sadly. He was afraid for her, but he knew she had to go in alone. Gerda put her arms round his neck. She thought she would never see him again.

She was alone, and there in front of her with its lofty blue towers was the palace of ice. The guards rushed up to kill her but she walked steadily towards them.

'Why should we let you in?' they shrieked around her.

'Because Kay is in there, and I love him.'

And they fell away from her like snowflakes.

Deep inside the palace, in the very heart of it, Kay sat and stared at his blocks of ice. The Snow Queen laughed at his efforts to solve her mystery.

'Are you satisfied with that? Try again, boy!'

He no longer had the strength to push the blocks around, but stared at them until his brain was as numb and cold as his body. His heart was like a fallen bird inside him, hardly fluttering.

And it was there that Gerda found him. He was blue with cold and his eyes were like glass, staring, just staring. 'Kay!' she shouted. She ran to him but he took no notice of her, as if he couldn't hear her or see her.

'Kay, Kay, it's me! Look at me. I can't tell if you're breathing.'

And still he took no notice of her, but stared at the blocks of ice.

'Kay, please speak to me! I've come all this way

to find you. They all thought you were dead, but I knew you weren't. I gave away my red shoes so I could find you. Don't you remember me at all?'

She put her arms round him. 'We count the roses on our tree. A rose for you, a rose for me,' she whispered. He turned his head slowly to look at her.

She tried again. 'We count the roses on our tree . . .'

'A rose for you, a rose for me!' he whispered, and at that moment he knew her. He started to cry, and the tears warmed his eyes and he could see her. His tears ran down into his heart and melted the ice around it.

Gerda pulled him to his feet and started to dance round with him to warm him up, and as they danced the blocks of ice began to move too, all on their own. They skated together to form a pattern of letters.

'Eternity. They're spelling Eternity!' Kay shouted. 'That's the mystery! I'm free, Gerda. I'm free!'

When the Snow Queen saw Gerda and Kay running hand in hand out of her palace what could she do but toss her head and laugh. They were nothing to her now. She was bored with her game. What did she understand about the power of love? What did the wicked imps know about friendship? Nothing.

Baa-baa was waiting for Gerda and Kay in the garden. He took them back to the Finn woman, and she gave them food for the rest of the journey. They met the Robber Girl in the forest, and they walked on until they came to where the

spring flowers were growing. They walked on to where the rivers were running free, and all the city bells were ringing. They were home.

They ran into the house and up the stairs, and there was the grandmother waiting for them with her hands in her lap as if they had never been away. They went to sit on the flower bridge, and laughed to find that their chairs were far too small for them now.

And it was summer again, in that place of long ago.

The Goose Girl

Retold by Gillian Cross

Illustrated by Peter Bailey

O nce there was a princess whose father was dead. She was promised in marriage to a king's son in a distant country, but she stayed in her mother's house until she was old enough to be a wife.

While she was growing up, her mother, the queen, collected a great store of treasure to go with her. There were rubies and diamonds and sapphires; necklaces of river pearls and goblets of golden filigree; rolls of Chinese

silk and carpets from the desert.

But the greatest treasure of all was a horse called Falada. He was a handsome and noble horse and, when the time was right, he could speak.

At last, the princess was old enough to leave and travel to her husband's country. Before she went, her mother called her in.

'I've given you many treasures to take with you,' the old queen said. 'But before you leave I'm going to give you one more thing, to protect you on your travels.'

She called to her maid in waiting.

'Bring me a white linen cloth.'

The maid brought the cloth and the queen took a needle and pricked her own finger until it bled. Holding her hand over the linen cloth, she let the blood drip, so that the white cloth was stained with three red drops.

'Keep this safe,' she said to her daughter, 'and nothing evil will be able to touch you.'

The princess took the cloth and hid it inside the front of her dress. Then she put on a rich travelling cloak and covered her face with a silk veil.

'Put on *your* cloak too,' the queen said to her maid. 'You're going with my daughter, to be her companion and carry her gold cup.'

The maid put on her rough woollen cloak and shabby white veil and followed the princess down to the courtyard. There was a train of pack-horses waiting there, loaded with treasure. And beside them was Falada, saddled up for the princess to ride.

'Fetch another horse for my maid,' the queen

called to the stable boys. 'She's going to travel with the princess.'

The stable boys thought it was a pity to send away another good horse, so they fetched a bony, broken-winded gelding from the stables and gave him to the maid.

When she and the princess had mounted, the queen said goodbye to her daughter and the two young women set off for the distant country where the prince lived.

They had not travelled very far when the princess began to feel thirsty, so she turned off the track and rode down into the trees beside the river. The maid followed, on her ugly old horse.

'Please get down,' said the princess, 'and fetch me some water in my gold cup. I'm very thirsty.'

Why should I do what she says? thought the maid. *There's no one to make me obey.*

So she said, 'Get down yourself if you want some water, and drink without your gold cup. I'm not going to be your slave!'

The princess was upset, but she saw that the maid was fierce and determined. *We have a long way to travel together,* she thought. *It's better not to quarrel.*

She slid off Falada's back and knelt down by the river, trying to look as though she didn't care. But as she stooped over to drink, she started to cry.

The three drops of blood heard her, and spoke from where she had them hidden.

'If your mother saw you now, it would break her heart.'

The maid looked down from her horse and

thought, *If it were not for those three drops of blood, I could overpower this princess and have what I long for.* But she knew the power of the linen cloth, and she didn't dare to touch the princess.

The princess mounted and they travelled on, but before long she was thirsty again and she rode down to the river, with the maid close behind her.

'Please get down,' said the princess, 'and fetch me some water in my gold cup. I'm so thirsty I shall die if I don't have a drink.'

'Why should I get down?' said the maid. 'There's water in the river. Go and drink it, if you're thirsty.'

So, for a second time, the princess dismounted from Falada and went down to the river, struggling to hide her tears. But she couldn't hide them from the drops of blood on the linen cloth.

They spoke to her again. 'If your mother saw

you now, it would break her heart.'

The maid heard them and scowled, thinking of what she longed to do. But she didn't dare to try.

Then, as the princess stooped over the river to drink, the linen cloth fell out of her dress. It floated away down the river, and was lost for ever.

The princess didn't see it fall, because she was stooping, but the maid saw, and her heart leaped. *My moment has come!* she thought. *The princess has lost the three drops of blood and now she will be too weak to defend herself.*

She slid quietly off her horse, and pulled a dagger out of her belt. Creeping up behind the princess, she caught hold of her long, golden hair and held the dagger to her throat.

'Take off all your fine clothes,' she hissed, 'and give them to me! Or I will kill you and throw you in the river.'

When the princess felt the knife blade against

her throat, she knew it was useless to struggle. She stripped off her rich cloak and her silk veil, and all her beautiful wedding garments.

'Take my old grey dress,' said the maid, 'and my cloak and veil. You must wear those now.'

So the two of them changed clothes in the trees by the river, with no one but the horses to see. Falada watched it all, but he did not speak.

When the maid was dressed in finery and draped with jewels, she pressed the point of the dagger against the princess's ribs.

'Now swear that you will never tell anyone what has happened here,' she said. 'If you don't swear, I'll stick this dagger into your heart and

leave you for the wolves to eat.'

The princess saw that she meant it, and she was very frightened. 'I swear that I will never tell a living soul,' she said.

The maid was triumphant. 'Now I am the mistress! And I shall be the prince's bride! You are the maid, and you can ride that ugly old horse. Falada is mine.'

Putting her foot in the stirrup, she jumped into the saddle and stuck her spurs into Falada's sides. The princess mounted the old horse and followed her, and that was how they travelled on to their destination.

At last they reached the country where the prince's father ruled. When they rode into the city, people ran along after them, shouting and cheering. The maid went haughtily through the crowds, but the princess rode with her head down and her eyes on the ground.

They passed under a great arched gateway and

clattered into the courtyard of the old king's castle. The prince hurried out to meet them. Seeing the maid, in her rich clothes, he thought that she was his promised bride, and he greeted her joyfully.

'Welcome to your new home!'

He did not even notice the shabby princess, who dismounted to hold the horses. He was longing to hear the voice of his bride. But all he got was a haughty nod as he lifted the maid down from her saddle.

The prince was disappointed, but he did not let it show. *She is tired,* he thought, *after her long journey.* Gently he took her hand.

'Come into the great tower,' he said. 'The king my father is waiting to meet you.'

The princess was left in the courtyard, holding the horses, while the maid swept off on the prince's arm. Falada saw it all, but still he did not speak.

Up in the tower, the old king was looking down

at the courtyard. He saw the princess, and she looked so humble and gentle that he wondered who she was.

'Tell me,' he said to the maid, when the prince had presented her, 'who is that young woman holding the horses?'

The maid tossed her head. 'She's not worthy of your notice, sire. She's a poor, ignorant girl who came to keep me company on the journey. Now that we're here, she needs some work to do, or she'll lounge around being a nuisance. Can you find her a job?'

Just at that moment, there was a loud noise of hissing and honking. A great flock of geese came under the arch and into the yard. They scattered everywhere, pecking at the servants' legs and annoying the horses. Running behind them was a boy in a feathered hat. He tried to round up the geese, but there were too many of them.

'Poor Conrad,' said the king. 'He has to drive

those geese to the meadows every morning and bring them back at night, but he finds it hard to control them. The girl in the courtyard can help him.'

'Excellent,' said the maid. 'It will suit her very well to be a goose girl.'

She curtsied and went off with the prince, to see the apartments set aside for her. They were beautiful rooms, with carved furniture and embroidered hangings. When she saw them, the maid was even more determined to keep the princess's place.

But through the window she caught sight of the horses in the courtyard. And she remembered that Falada could speak, when the time was right.

Who knows when that will be? she thought. *If he tells what he saw in the trees by the river, I shall lose everything.*

Turning round, she gave the prince a false, wheedling smile. 'Will you do me a favour?' she

said. 'To celebrate our meeting.'

'Anything you like,' said the prince.

The maid pointed through the window. 'Do you see those horses in the courtyard? The big horse looks noble and handsome, but he's a foul, ill-tempered brute. I rode him on my journey here, and he threw me to the ground three times. Please send him to the knacker's to be killed, so he can't give me any more trouble.'

The prince had not expected anything like that, and he was upset by the idea of killing such a fine-looking horse. But he would not break his promise. Calling a servant, he gave orders that Falada should go to the knacker's.

Immediately, the servant went down to the courtyard and took charge of both the horses. The princess thought they were going to be fed and groomed, so she handed them over gladly. But only the ugly old gelding went to the stables. Falada was led off to the knacker's, straight away. And still he did not speak.

By the time the maid sat down to dinner, he was dead.

When the princess found out what had happened, she felt that her heart would break. *My only friend has gone,* she thought. *Falada was the only one who knew about me.*

She couldn't bear to be so alone. That night she took the few gold coins she had in her purse and slipped out of the castle. Going under the great arched gateway, she crept down to the lower part of the city and went to visit the knacker's man.

'Today you killed a fine horse from the castle,' she said. 'If I give you this gold, will you nail up

his head in the arch of the great gateway?'

She knew she would walk under that arch every day now that she was a goose girl. That was the way Conrad drove the geese out to the meadows.

The knacker's man thought it was a strange request, but he promised to do as she asked. The princess gave him the gold and crept back to the castle.

Next morning, as the sun was coming up, she and Conrad set out for the meadows, driving the geese between them. As they passed under the great dark gateway, the princess looked up into the shadows, high above. There was Falada's head nailed to the wall.

She nearly fainted with grief. With tears running down her face, she called up to him.

'Falada, O alas, alas,
That you should hang there as I pass.'

Then, at last, Falada spoke. From the darkness, a faint voice drifted down as the head answered her.

'And O alas, alas, Princess
That you should pass in such distress.'

Then the geese hissed and Conrad shouted, and the princess walked on under the archway.

When they reached the meadows, the geese wandered about to feed on the grass. Sitting down on a stone, the princess untied her hair, so that she could comb it. As she shook it out the sun caught it, and Conrad saw that it was pure gold.

I want some of that golden hair, he thought.

He was sure the princess would never give him any, so he waited until she started combing it and singing to herself. Then he crept up behind her. He was planning to snatch a hair before she could stop him.

But the princess saw his shadow creeping up on her and she changed her song. Pulling the comb through her hair, she sang to the wind:

> 'Blow wind
> over stone
> for a princess all alone.
> Blow wind
> over water
> to protect a queen's daughter.
> Blow wind
> wild and free
> to keep harm far from me.'

Immediately, there was a great gust of wind.

Conrad's feathered hat was snatched off his head and it went tumbling over the grass. He ran after it as fast as he could, but the wind blew it here and there all around the meadows.

By the time he caught it, the princess had plaited her hair tightly and pinned it close to her head, and he had no chance of stealing even a single hair.

He was so angry that he sulked all day and refused to speak to her.

The next day, they walked out with the geese again, and when the princess went under the archway and saw Falada's head she called up to him again.

'Falada, O alas, alas,
That you should hang there as I pass.'

Again the head answered her from high in the shadows and Conrad heard it and sulked,

kicking at the cobbles.

When they reached the meadows, Conrad wandered off. He pretended to look at the geese, but really he was waiting for the princess to take out her comb. When she untied her hair, he started sneaking up behind her. This time, he was determined to steal a golden hair.

But the princess heard his footsteps in the grass. Pulling the comb through her hair, she sang to the wind again:

> *'Blow wind*
> *over stone*
> *for a princess all alone.*
> *Blow wind*
> *over water*
> *to protect a queen's daughter.*
> *Blow wind*
> *wild and free*
> *to keep harm far from me.'*

309

The moment she finished singing, the wind blew out of nowhere, twitching Conrad's hat away. It went spinning towards the river and he had to run hard to save it from falling into the water.

When he came back, the princess's hair was twisted close to her head and fixed with combs and pins. Conrad was too angry to speak. He stumped up and down the meadows, working out how to get his revenge.

When they returned to the castle, he demanded to see the king.

'Sire,' he said, 'you must take away that girl you sent to herd the geese with me. I can't work with her.'

The old king was amazed. 'Why not? She looks gentle and quiet enough.'

'She is not gentle or quiet,' Conrad said. 'She is strange and troublesome. When we go out in the morning, she talks to the horse's head that is nailed up in the great archway. And the head talks back to her.'

That sounded more than strange to the king and he began to wonder about the goose girl. 'Is that all she does?'

'No, it isn't,' said Conrad. 'When we're in the meadows, she sings to the wind. And the wind blows my hat away.'

That sounded even stranger. The king decided that he had to see these things for himself.

'Put up with the girl for one more day,' he said. 'If you still complain after that, I will find her some other work.'

Grudgingly, Conrad agreed.

In the morning, he and the princess set out

again with the geese. But this time the old king was behind, following them secretly. As they walked under the great gateway, he saw the goose girl look up into the shadows, high above. And he heard her say:

> *'Falada, O alas, alas,*
> *That you should hang there as I pass.'*

From out of the darkness came an answering voice that made the king's hair stand on end.

> *'And O alas, alas, Princess*
> *That you should pass in such distress.'*

This is even stranger than I was told, thought the king. And he crept on behind the geese.

When they reached the meadows, the princess loosened her hair and began to comb it. The king saw that her hair was all of gold, and he saw Conrad creeping up behind her, to steal a hair. But before he was near enough to snatch at one, the princess felt the grass rustle, and she started to sing.

At the sound of her voice, the wind began to blow. In a moment, Conrad's hat was tweaked off his head and it went sailing across the meadow and out on to the river. Conrad had to wade in, up to his knees, to get it back.

The old king watched the goose girl plaiting her hair and pinning it round her head. *She is a good, modest girl*, he thought,

but there is a mystery here.

When the geese came back in the evening, the king sent a servant to fetch the goose girl. She came in her shabby old clothes, for she had no others.

'I saw two strange things today,' said the king. 'First, I saw you talk to a horse's head in the archway, and I heard it answer you. Then, when you sang in the meadows, the wind came from nowhere and blew off Conrad's hat. Tell me who you are, and why the horse's head called you "Princess".'

'I'm sorry, sire,' said the princess, 'but I can't tell you that.'

'I am the king, and I command you to tell me!'

'I can't,' the princess said. 'I swore a solemn oath never to tell the story to anyone.'

'You *shall* tell me! If you don't, I will have you beaten and locked up!'

The princess began to cry, but she wouldn't

break her promise, even though the king threatened her with worse punishments, to test her.

When he saw how true and faithful she was, he liked her even better than before. 'Don't cry, my dear,' he said. 'I won't make you break your oath. But I can see that you want to tell the secret.'

'Indeed I do!' the princess cried. 'But I can never tell you, or any living soul, for that is what I swore.'

Then the king saw a way to rescue her from her oath, without forcing her to break it. He pointed to the great iron stove in the corner of the room. In winter, huge logs were burnt inside it, but now it was empty for the summer.

'Creep in there,' he said, 'and tell your secret to the stove. That isn't a living soul.'

The princess crept into the stove and pulled the door shut behind her. Then she started to wail and cry.

'Alas,' she said. 'If my mother the queen could see me now, she would die of grief. She sent me here to be the prince's wife, but my wicked maid forced me to change clothes with her. Now she is the bride and I am only the goose girl. Alas, alas!'

As she spoke, her voice boomed and echoed inside the iron stove. The king heard every word.

He sent a servant to find the prince and then he opened the door of the stove and called to the princess.

'Come out, my dear, and let me talk to you.'

He and the prince asked her complicated questions about her family, and about the country where she was born, and she answered every one.

When they saw that she was indeed the true

bride, the king was delighted. And the prince wept for joy to find that his wife was this humble, gentle girl, and not the arrogant and overbearing maid.

'Tonight,' said the king, 'there is a great feast to celebrate the wedding. By the end of the feast, you will have your rightful place. And the false bride will have chosen her own punishment.'

Then the princess was given splendid clothes and jewels, and a place was set for her at the wedding feast. The maid was at the feast too, sitting at the high table, next to the prince, but she was so proud and haughty that she did not once look at the modest princess.

When the feast was nearly over, the old king spoke to the false bride. 'I have to judge the case of a disloyal servant,' he said. 'Instead of looking after her mistress, she threatened to kill her, and stole all her possessions. How do you think I should punish someone like that?'

The maid was flattered that he asked her opinion. 'A treacherous servant deserves the worst punishment,' she said grandly. 'This woman should be shut into a barrel full of nails and dragged through the streets by horses, until she is dead!'

The king stood up. 'You shall have your wish!' he said, in a terrible voice. 'For you are that servant, and here is the mistress you betrayed!'

Stepping down into the hall, he went to the true princess and took her hand. 'Come up to your rightful place,' he said. 'You are the prince's real wife. The false bride shall have the punishment she chose.'

The guards dragged the maid away to meet her fate and the princess stepped on to the dais to take her place beside the prince. He loved her twice as much because she had once been a goose girl, and so they celebrated their marriage, and lived happily every after.

Rumpelstiltskin

Retold by Kit Wright
Illustrated by Ted Dewan

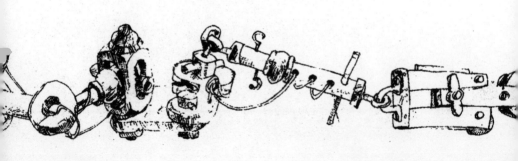

There was once an old miller who lived deep in the forest by a winding river. And he had a beautiful daughter named Isabella, whom he loved more than the breath in his body, more than his own life.

But the miller was poor.

Every day he sighed to himself, 'If only I were a rich man, and could give Isabella the life of a fine lady!'

They both worked very hard at the mill,

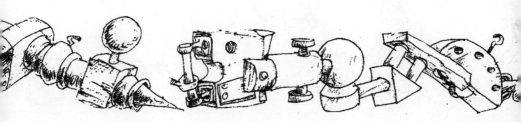

grinding the corn into meal to make bread. Round and round turned the huge wheel in the rushing water. Slowly inside the mill, the wooden cogs creaked, and the shaft spun, and the great stone went groaning round.

It was like an elephant dancing on the bank!

One day a Prince came riding through the forest. The sun shone through the canopy of the leaves, making a light like underwater. The birds sang and the Prince sang, for he was handsome and happy.

Then he came out of the trees and on to the river bank into broad sunlight. He reined in his horse and the tinkle of its harness died.

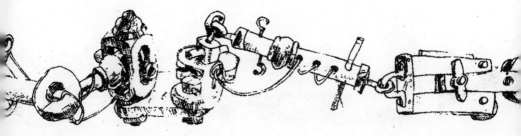

The only sounds were the water and the pounding of the mill.

But the Prince wasn't listening. He was looking.

For there stood Isabella, and she was the most beautiful sight the Prince had ever seen.

He swung down from his white horse.

'Beautiful lady, tell me who you are!'

'Why, I am Isabella, sir. My father is the miller.'

And the Prince didn't have long to wait to meet him. Hearing them talk, he came running out. He was very jealous about his daughter, and didn't like her speaking to strange men.

'Who—'

And the miller's voice stopped in his throat. For the man standing in front of him was a Prince in all his majesty and finery.

'S-sir, forgive me!'

'Nothing to forgive, sir. Your daughter is the most beautiful girl in the world. That's what I wanted to tell her.'

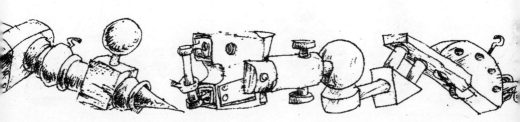

'Ah,' said the miller. 'Ah . . .'

Now this is where he made his great mistake. The Prince had fallen in love with Isabella the moment he saw her. He wanted to marry her. But the old man didn't know this.

Remember he loved his daughter more than the breath in his body, more than his own life. He wanted the very best for her, and this was a golden chance. So he said:

'She is not only beautiful, sir. She is clever enough to do anything.'

'For instance?'

The old man racked his brains and he heard himself say:

'She can spin straw into gold!'

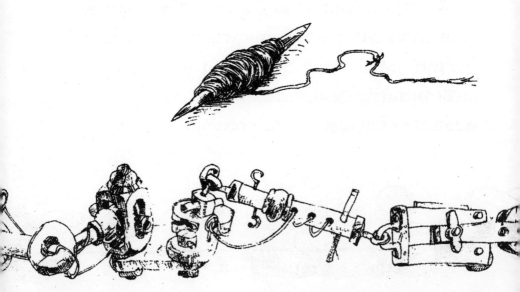

Then the Prince rode back on his white horse through the forest, with the leaves whistling against his arms and shoulders. In the palace, there was the King.

'Fool of a boy! Where have you been?'

Well, the King was of course his father, and a very nasty old piece of work indeed. He was rich, richer than anyone, but not rich enough for himself. He wanted more.

'Where have you been, fool of a boy?'

So the Prince told him.

'Father, I've been in the forest and down by the riverside. There I met the most beautiful girl in the world, the daughter of the miller. Her name is Isabella, and I want to make her my wife.'

'Wife? You want to make a *miller's* daughter your wife? Millers are poor, you idiot! What has she got?'

'Beautiful eyes like the stars.'

'Stars? They are worth nothing.'

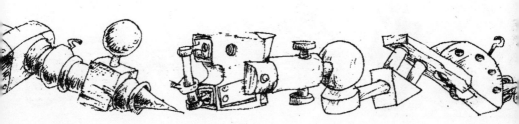

'Wonderful skin like the snow.'

'Snow? That's worth even less.'

And the poor Prince thought that what he had loved in Isabella was the shining of her spirit by the water.

But that wouldn't do.

So he said: 'She can spin straw into gold.'

Well, the King was always angry, but now he was *furious*.

'Drivelling dunderhead! Nobody ever born can turn straw into gold! Get out of my sight!'

But a couple of days later, he found himself wondering. He was drinking a cup of horrible wine, because he was too mean to have anything nicer.

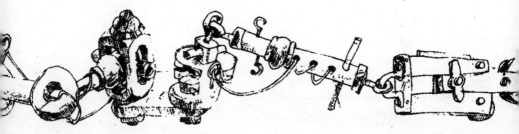

And he wondered.

He wondered over his horrible wine.

Straw into gold, straw into gold.

The idea was quite ridiculous, of course. But just supposing . . .

Why, he would have more gold than there was water in the sea!

He sent for his nastiest servant, a man named Grinling. The hairs that grew in Grinling's ears stood out about a foot on either side.

'Grinling,' said the King, 'go through the forest. Get to the riverside. Find there the beautiful daughter of a miller. Her name is Isabella.'

'Yes, your majesty.'

'Yes indeed, Grinling. And Grinling?'

'Yes, your majesty?'

'Bring her back before nightfall. Or else I'll grind your bones into wine!'

So Grinling didn't take long to find Isabella. He dragged her back, and the old miller stood

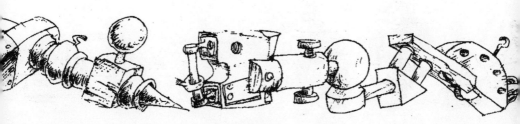

weeping on the bank, knowing he'd told a lie.

For of course Isabella couldn't spin straw into gold, any more than she could spin gold into straw. She loved her father dearly, but how she wished he hadn't been so rash! Now she was frightened to say she could, and frightened to say she couldn't.

The crafty old eyes of the King were each like the tongue of a snake.

'So you are Isabella. Well, I see you are as beautiful as they say.'

He sniggered.

'But beauty is quite useless, my dear. Quite useless. It won't even save your life!'

And he laughed loud and long, so his belly shook.

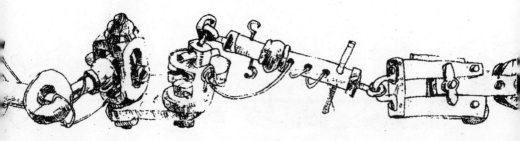

Now his eyes were burning.

'I understand you have a remarkable gift. We are going to put it to the test. Aren't we, Grinling?'

And Grinling, who was skulking by the side of the throne, said, 'Yes indeed, your majesty!'

'Yes indeed, Grinling. Now, my dear. If you can do what they say you can do, well and good. And if you can't, well . . . *not so good.*'

And the King spread out his hand like a blade and drew it across his throat.

'Do I make myself clear?'

Isabella trembled.

'Spin straw into gold by morning, and you shall marry my son. Fail and I fear, my dear . . .'

His shoulders wobbled, his mouth twitched.

'Fail, and I fear, my dear . . . you won't be marrying anyone ever at all! Take her away, Grinling!'

And as she was led up the stone stairway, the last sound Isabella heard was the King, howling

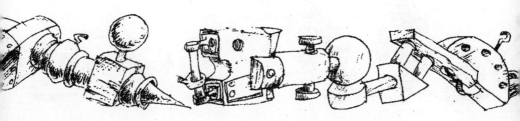

and hooting and shrieking with laughter on his throne.

She looked round the room where Grinling had locked her. There was a stool, a spinning wheel and a huge pile of straw.

The spinning wheel reminded her of the great mill wheel at home, that dipped and plunged and rolled in the rolling water. How happy she had been with her silly old father!

And she thought of the day the Prince came riding by. He was handsome. He was kind. And she had fallen in love with his spirit, shining by the water.

She looked out of the window.

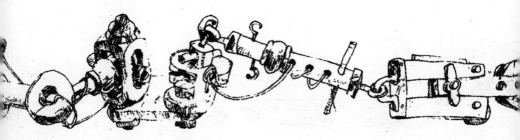

It was miles to the ground.

And she couldn't spin straw into anything!

She plunged her head into her hands and wept bitterly.

Then she heard a creak. She looked up. Outside the window was a high oak tree with spreading branches. And on one of them stood the strangest creature Isabella had ever seen.

It was a little man. He'd a head like a knobbly potato . . . and huge feet!

'Do not cry, little maiden,' he said, in a voice like two rough stones being scraped against each other. 'Open the window.'

Poor Isabella had nothing to lose. So she did as he said.

He jumped on to the window ledge and down into the room.

'Well, little maiden. Things don't look very promising.'

She stared at him.

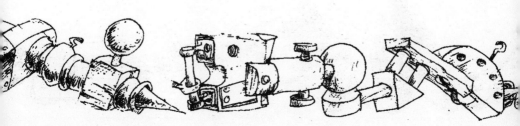

'I rather think they want you to spin that pile of straw into gold by the morning. Am I right?'

'How did you know?'

'I know everything,' said the little man.

'Who are you?'

'Ah! Now that would be telling!'

And he laughed louder than you would have thought that such a small creature could.

'It doesn't seem funny to *me*,' said Isabella, and began to weep again.

'Do not cry, little maiden, do not cry. I am here to help you.'

'How can you do that? Nobody can!'

'I'll spin your straw into gold. But nothing comes for nothing, little maiden. What will you give me to do it?'

'I've nothing to give you!'

'How about your necklace?'

And Isabella's hand flew to her throat. Her necklace was the only gift her poor father had

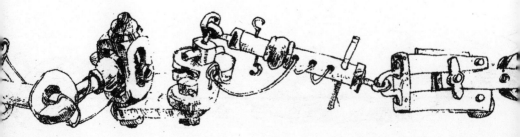

been able to give her. It made her sad to think of losing it. And she didn't really believe that the little man could help her. But she had no choice.

'I will give you my necklace.'

'Done.'

And with one of his huge and hairy feet, the little man took a tremendous BOOT at the spinning wheel!

Goodness, how he could kick!

The wheel went hurtling round. It rocked and swayed on its base, then settled into a whirr. It spun so fast that it didn't seem to be moving at all! And on the other side of the straw, a river of gold came pouring down till a great yellow mountain rose against the wall.

Solid gold!

'Oh, thank you, thank you, thank you!' cried Isabella.

But the little man had his hand out.

She gave him the necklace.

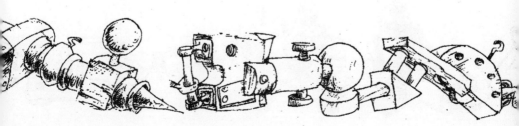

Then she turned again to look at the glinting treasure.

'How did you—'

But he had gone.

So when the King and Grinling burst into the room in the morning, they were amazed.

'This is a *fine* day, Grinling!'

'Yes, your majesty.'

'Yes indeed, Grinling! Run and get me a giant cup of my bonemeal wine to celebrate! For I shall be the richest man there has ever been in the world!'

When they were down in the hall, Isabella said:

'Can I please marry the Prince now? I've done everything you wanted, your majesty.'

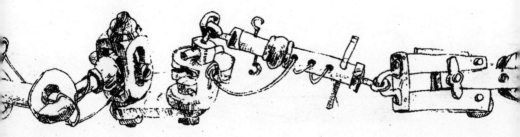

'Ah. Well. *Ah*.'

And the King's crafty old eyes were like the tongues of snakes.

Grinling stood and waggled the hair in his ears.

'My dear, that was all very well as far as it went,' said the King. 'Indeed, it was quite impressive. But how do we know it wasn't a flash in the pan? You must do it again tonight, and *then* you shall marry my son!'

And again Isabella was locked in the room with the spinning wheel, the stool and an even bigger pile of straw.

Again she plunged her head into her hands and bitterly she wept.

Outside a great wind was blowing. The oak tree shivered and rocked as though it would take off from the ground! She looked up and she saw a big dark bird flapping towards her in the mighty wind. And it landed on the window ledge.

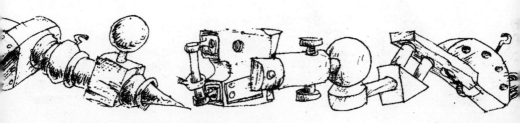

But it wasn't a bird . . . it was the little man!

'Do not cry, little maiden, do not cry. Open the window.'

And when he was inside, he said, 'All to do again I see, little maiden! What will you give me this time? For nothing comes for nothing.'

'But I have nothing to give you!'

'What about your ring?'

And Isabella rubbed the ring on her finger. It had been her mother's, and it was the only thing she had left to remember her by. She would be sad to lose it. But she had no choice.

'I will give you my ring.'

'Done!'

And with one of his huge, hairy feet he took a tremendous BOOT at the spinning wheel!

Again the river of gold poured down and the yellow mountain rose from the floor.

'Oh, thank you, thank you, thank you!' cried Isabella.

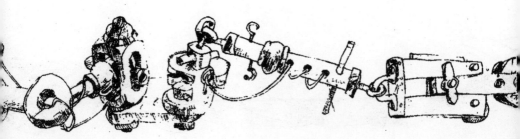

But the little man had his hand out.

She gave him the ring.

He was gone.

Well, the King was even more delighted when he burst in with Grinling in the morning.

'Can I please marry the Prince now?' said Isabella.

'Ah,' said the King. '*Ah*. Now, all the best things come in threes, my dear. That makes them true. And just to make sure you haven't been lucky twice . . . do it again tonight! And then you shall marry my son.'

And they locked her in . . . with a pile of straw so big it almost filled the room!

That night a terrible storm shook the palace.

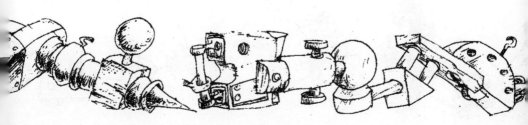

Thunder boomed and bellowed, lightning zig-zagged down the sky. But Isabella kept the window open, hoping the little man would come again.

And he did, sliding right into the room down a ladder of lightning.

'I've *nothing* to give you this time,' cried Isabella, 'nothing at all!'

'But you will have, little maiden. Oh, you will have.'

'What do you mean?'

'You will marry your handsome Prince.'

'How do you know?'

'I know everything. And after a time your first child will be born. But . . .'

And the little man gave a rasping laugh from his knobbly potato head.

'You won't have it for long. You'll give it to *me*!'

Isabella stared at him.

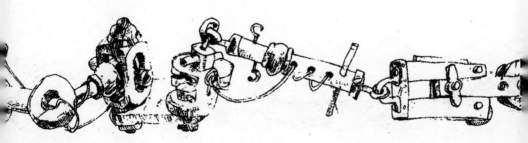

'I gave you my necklace, I gave you my ring . . . you cannot take my child!'

'Nothing comes for nothing, little maiden. You have no choice.'

And she didn't.

In the morning there stood the glittering yellow mountain.

And this time the King did set her free. He felt he was sure of being the richest man there had ever been in the world!

And Isabella married the Prince. They had a wonderful wedding in the mountains. After a time their first child was born. And they were very happy.

They didn't have to worry about the King. He

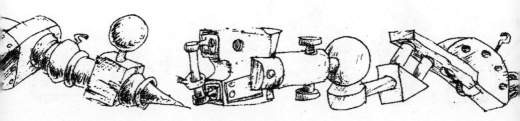

spent all day and night in his store-room, running his fingers over and over the shining piles of gold. He howled and hooted and shrieked with laughter, drinking cup after cup of his horrible bonemeal wine. One day he exploded, and that was the end of him.

But, of course, they had someone to fear.

And sure enough, one night he came.

And this time he didn't jump off a tree, or fly like a bird, or slide down a ladder of lightning. He walked on his huge feet up the stone stairway, slowly into the room where Isabella was rocking her baby in the cradle.

'Give me your child.'

'Oh please,' said Isabella, 'please!'

And she wept twice as bitterly as she had ever wept in her life.

A funny look came over the little man's knobbly potato face. He grinned, and then he laughed with his rasping laugh.

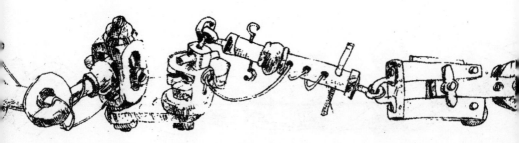

'All right, I'll give you a chance. That might be fun!'

'What do you mean?'

'This. If you can discover my name within three days, then you shall keep your child. If not . . . well, of course . . . *not*!'

And he was gone.

Well, of course Isabella told her husband every-thing, and he was very sad.

What could they do?

The Prince summoned the palace knights. Their names were these: Ronald the Bold, Vernon the Bald, Sidney the Big and Denzil the Bigger.

And they were as lazy and useless a bunch as you could hope to find.

'We have three days,' said the Prince, 'to find out the little man's name. And that means finding *him*. Ride up into the mountains. Ride out into the forest. Go far and wide, search high and low and bring me back his name.'

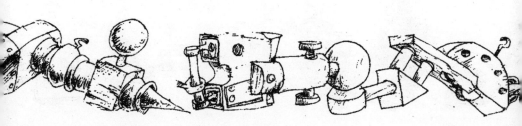

'You can count on me,' said Ronald the Bold.

'Consider it done,' said Vernon the Bald.

'Just leave it to us,' said Sidney the Big and Denzil the Bigger.

It was winter now. In the freezing wind the trees were heavily piled with snow and the paths were coated with tongues of ice.

The knights were not enjoying themselves at all. They soon decided they'd had enough, so they made for a woodman's abandoned hut and sat there playing cards all day.

'We'll just make up some names,' said Vernon the Bald.

And they all agreed. So that evening they told them to the Prince, who told them to Isabella.

Late that night, she felt the stone stairs shudder with the little man's footsteps.

'Well? And what is my name?'

'Is it Boris?'

'It is not.'

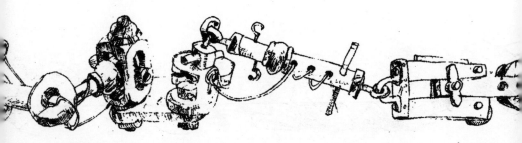

'Is it Bernard Belvedere?'

'It is not.'

'Is it Brian Broderick Brewhouse Baraimian?'

'No!' cried the little man, 'it is none of those things!'

And he laughed, loud and harsh.

'You will never guess it! Two nights more, and the child in that cradle is *mine*!'

He was gone.

And Isabella wept.

The next day the knights didn't bother to look at all. They took some bottles of the King's bonemeal wine and headed straight for the woodman's hut.

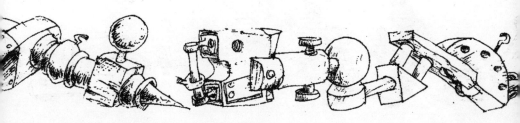

'My goodness, this wine is horrible,' said Ronald.

'No wonder the King was so nasty,' said Vernon.

'No wonder he exploded,' said Sidney and Denzil.

And they made up some more names.

The Prince told them to Isabella.

Late that night, there was the little man.

'Well, can you tell me my name?'

'Is it Peveril?'

'It is not.'

'Is it Peregrine Pighurst?'

'It is not.'

'Is it Patrick Prendergast Petunia Junior?'

'No, it is none of those stupid, ridiculous names.'

And this time he didn't laugh. The eyes in his knobbly potato face were as hard as the ice outside the palace walls.

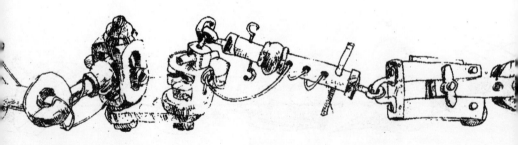

'This is no game. Tomorrow night you will look your last on your child.'

He was gone.

And bitterly, bitterly, Isabella wept.

The next day was the last day.

The knights did nothing.

But three men never gave up, as the whirling flakes fell thicker than ever. One was, of course, the Prince. He rode like the wind under the mountain overhangs, white horse like a snowstorm in a snowstorm. They staggered on through the deepest drifts and they crept up icy ledges. But nowhere did he see the little man, or hear any word of him.

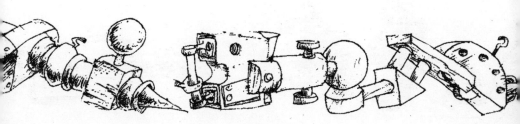

The second was the old miller, who loved his daughter more than the breath in his body, more than his own life. He wanted to save her child. Of course he lived in the palace now, and the great mill wheel stood rusting in the frozen river. He trudged along the silent bank, hoping to hear some word of the little man. But no one he ever saw knew anything at all.

And there was a third.

This was a man who had loved Isabella from the very first moment he saw her. And he had hurt her.

He didn't want that. He wanted her to be happy. When at last she married the Prince, the man had been overjoyed. And now he was crawling and scrambling through thorns and under-growth, through brambles and whipping bushes. His skin bled and his eyes stung as he looked for the little man.

Do you know who it was?

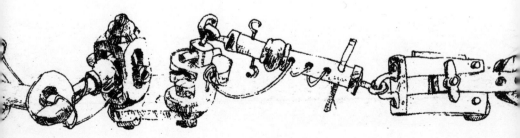

It was . . .

GRINLING!

For Grinling wasn't a bad person at all. Early in his life, he'd been captured by the King, who made him his slave. He'd always had hairy ears, of course, but the King had made him grow them out for ever, like sideways horns. Or else he'd grind poor Grinling's bones into wine.

And he heard someone singing.

A harsh, low, rasping song, such as he'd never heard in all of his life.

He crept behind a tree.

He felt the touch of hands on his back. But he knew they were friendly. He knew they were the old hands of the miller, and the young hands of the Prince.

No one dared breathe.

Down in a clearing of the forest, a fire was burning brightly. And round and round it danced none other than the little man!

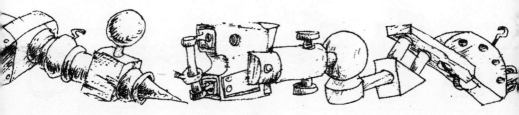

As he danced he sang:

'Crackle, logs, and stars, be dumb,
Tonight a royal child will come.
They'll never beat me at my game,
For RUMPELSTILTSKIN is my name!'

Softly the three watchers stole away through the snow.

That night, everyone in the palace was waiting and whispering, when they felt the shudder of footsteps on the stairway.

'Well?' said the little man.

'Oh,' said Isabella. 'It's you again. Now, tell

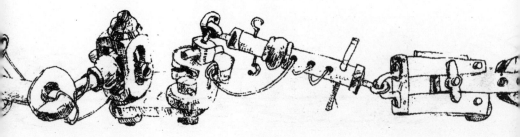

me. Could your name be Tim?'

'It is not,' he sneered.

'Is it Jim?'

'It is not.'

And this time he grinned from ear to ear.

'Oh well, then,' said Isabella, gently rocking the cradle with her foot, 'I suppose it must be Rumpelstiltskin.'

The little man's face froze like the ice on the mountains. Then it split in a great bellow of rage that shook the palace walls. He lifted a huge, hairy foot and he STAMPED!

He stamped so hard he went through the floor, and through the floor under that, and through the basement. He stamped so hard he went down, down, down, to the centre of the earth.

And nobody ever saw him again.

The Prince and Isabella had many more children. On summer days, they walk with them through the forest and down to the riverside. The

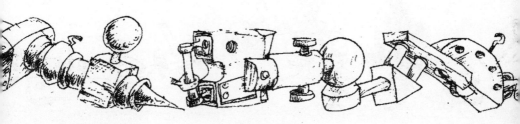

great mill wheel is again turning, for the lazy knights have to work there by the water.

The cogs creak, and the shaft spins, and the great stone goes grinding round.

It's like an elephant dancing . . . for joy!

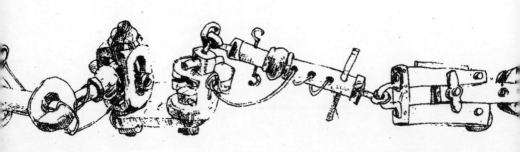

Cockadoodle-doo, Mr Sultana!

Retold by Michael Morpurgo

Illustrated by Michael Foreman

In a far-off Eastern land, a long, long time ago, there once lived a great and mighty Sultan. He was, without doubt, the richest, laziest, greediest and fattest Sultan there had ever been. He was so rich his palace was built of nothing but shining marble and glowing gold, so rich that even the buttons on his silken clothes were made of diamonds. He was so lazy he had to have a special servant to brush his teeth for him, and another one to wash him, and

another one to dress him.

He did nothing for himself, except eat. He was so greedy that every meal – breakfast, lunch and dinner – he'd gobble down a nice plump peacock just to himself, and then a great bowl of sweetmeats, too. And then he'd wash it all down with a jug of honeyed camel's milk.

It was because he was so very lazy and so very greedy that he was so very, very fat. He had to sleep in a bed wide enough for five grown men, and his pantaloons were the baggiest, most capacious pantaloons ever made for anyone anywhere.

But believe it or not there was something the Sultan cared about even more than his food – his treasure. He loved his treasure above anything else in the whole world.

Before he went to sleep every night, he would always open his treasure chest and count out his jewels – emeralds, rubies, diamonds, pearls,

sapphires, hundreds and hundreds of them – just to be quite sure they were all still there. Only then could he go to bed happy and sleep soundly.

But outside the walls of his palace, the Sultan's people lived like slaves, poor, wretched and hungry. They had to work every hour God gave them. And why? To keep the Sultan rich in jewels. Everything they harvested – their corn, their grapes, their figs, their dates, their pomegranates – all had to be given to the Sultan. He allowed them just enough food to keep body and soul together – no more.

One fine morning, the Sultan was out hunting. He loved to hunt, because all he had to do was sit astride his horse and send the hawks off to do the

hunting. There was only one horse in the land strong enough to carry him, a great stout old warhorse. But strong though he was, to be sat on by the great fat Sultan for hour after hour under the hot, hot sun, proved too much even for him.

Lathered up and exhausted, the old warhorse staggered suddenly and stumbled, throwing the Sultan to the ground. It took ten servants to get him to his feet and brush him down. He wasn't badly hurt, just a bit bumped and bruised, but he was angry; very angry. He ordered his servants to whip the old horse soundly, so that he wouldn't do it again. Then they all helped him back up on his horse, which took some time, of course; and off they went back to the palace.

The Sultan didn't know it, not yet, and no more did anyone else, but he'd left something behind lying in the dirt on the dusty farmyard track, something that had popped off his waist-coat when he'd fallen from his horse. It was a button, a shining, glittering diamond button.

Just a little way off, down the farmyard track, was a tumbledown farmhouse where there lived a poor old woman. She had little enough in this world – though she never complained of it – only a couple of nanny goats for her milk, a few hens for her eggs *and* a little red rooster. She always kept the goats hidden away inside her house, and the hens too, for fear that the Sultan's servants might come by and steal them away for the Sultan.

She had always tried to keep her little red rooster in the house too, because she loved him dearly, and because she wanted him to keep her

hens happy. But this was a little red rooster with a mind of its own, and whenever he could, he would go running off to explore the big, wide world outside, to find friends – and to find food, for he was always very hungry.

That same day, when the poor old woman went out to fetch water for her goats and hens, the little red rooster scooted out from under her skirts. Before she could stop him he was out through the open door and running off down the farm track.

'Come back, Little Red Rooster!' cried the poor old woman. 'Come back! If the Sultan finds you, he'll catch you and eat you up. Come back!'

But the little red rooster had never in his life been frightened of anything or anyone. He just

kept on running. 'Catch me if you can, mistress mine,' he called out.

On and on he ran, until he came to the farm track where the cornfield and the vineyard met. He knew this was just the perfect place to scratch around for a good meal. Here he'd find all the ripe corn and dried-up sultanas he could eat. As he pecked about busily in the earth, he came across dozens of wriggling worms and singing cicadas and burrowing beetles, but he never ate these. After all, these were his friends. He couldn't eat his friends – though he had thought about it once or twice.

Meanwhile, back in his gold and marble palace, the great Sultan was stamping up and down. He was in a horrible temper, his stomachs and his chins wobbling with fury.

'The diamond button off my waistcoat,' he roared. 'I have lost my diamond button. Search, you miserable beggars, search everywhere, every

nook and cranny.' His servants were scurrying here and there and everywhere, all over the palace, but they could not find it anywhere.

'I'll lop off your heads if you don't find it,' he bellowed. But no matter how loud he shouted, how terrible the threats, no one could find the missing diamond button.

'Am I surrounded by nothing but fools and imbeciles?' he thundered. 'I see I shall have to find it for myself. We shall go back and search every inch of ground we hunted over this morning. And you will go in front of me, all of you on your knees in the dust where you belong, and search for my diamond button. Fetch me my horse.' He clapped his hands. 'At once. At once.'

Out in the countryside, the little red rooster was scratching around in the dusty farm track at the edge of the cornfield. He scratched and he scratched. Suddenly there was something strange in the earth, something different, something very pretty that glistened and shone and twinkled in the sun. He tried eating it, but it didn't taste very good. So he dropped it. And then he had a sudden and brilliant idea.

'I know,' he said to himself. 'Poor old mistress mine loves pretty things. She's always saying so, and she's got nothing pretty of her own. I'll take it home for her. Then she won't be cross with me for running away, will she?'

But just as he picked it up again, along the farm track came the great fat Sultan on his horse, and in front of him, dozens of his servants, all of them crawling on their hands and knees in the dirt. Closer and closer they came. All at once they spotted the little red rooster *and* the diamond

button too, glinting in his beak.

'There, my lord Sultan!' they cried. 'Look! That little red rooster. He's got your diamond button.'

'So that's what it is,' the little red rooster said to himself.

The great fat Sultan rode up, scattering his servants hither and thither as he came. 'Little Red Rooster,' he said from high up on his horse. 'I see you have my diamond button. I am your great and mighty Sultan. Give it to me at once. It's valuable, very valuable. And it's mine.'

'I don't think so, Mr Sultana,' replied the little red rooster, who had never in his life been frightened of anyone or anything. 'Cockadoodle-doo, Mr Sultana. Finders keepers. If it's so valuable, then I'm going to give it to poor old mistress mine. She needs it a lot more than you, I think. Sorry, Mr Sultana.'

'What!' spluttered the Sultan. 'Mr Sultana?

How dare you speak to me like that? How dare you? Did you hear what that infernal bird called me? Fetch me that rooster. Fetch me my diamond button! Grab him! Grab that rooster!'

There was a frightful kerfuffle of dust and feathers and squawking, as the Sultan's servants tried to grab the little red rooster. Whatever they did, they just could not catch him. In the end, the little red rooster ran off into the cornfield. But although he'd escaped their clutches, he was very cross with himself, for in all the kerfuffle he had dropped the diamond button.

One of the Sultan's servants found it lying in the dust and brought it back to the Sultan. The

Sultan was delighted, of course, and all his servants were mightily relieved, too. Now, at least, none of them would have their heads lopped off, not that day anyway.

But had the Sultan seen the last of the little red rooster? Not by any means. The little red rooster wasn't going to give up that easily – he wasn't like that. He followed the Sultan and his servants back to the palace. Then, in the middle of the night, as everyone slept, he flew up to the Sultan's window, perched on the window-ledge, took a deep breath and crowed, and crowed. He let out the loudest, longest cockadoodle-doo he'd ever doodled in all his life.

'Cockadoodle-doo, Mr Sultana,' he crowed. 'Cockadoodle-doo!'

The Sultan tried to cover his ears. It didn't work.

'Cockadoodle-doo, Mr Sultana!'

The Sultan tried to bury his head in his pillow.

It didn't work.

'Cockadoodle-doo, Mr Sultana! Give me back my diamond button.'

By now the Sultan was in a terrible rage. He had had quite enough of this. He called in his servants. 'Grab me that infernal bird,' he cried. 'I know what I'll do. I know. We'll throw him in the well and drown him. That should shut him up, and shut him up for good.'

All night long, the Sultan and his servants chased around the palace after the little red rooster. The little red rooster had lots of fun. He played hide-and-seek behind the peacocks. He flew, he hopped, he ran. He perched on cornices, on chandeliers, on the Sultan's throne itself! And

that was where they finally caught him. One of the servants crept up behind and grabbed him by his tail feathers.

The little red rooster didn't really mind – he'd had enough of the game anyway. He wasn't at all frightened of water. He knew what to do with water. He wasn't worried.

'Aha!' cried the exultant Sultan. 'We've got you now. You've crowed your very last doodle-doo.'

'I don't think so, Mr Sultana,' said the little red rooster. But the Sultan took him by the neck and dropped him down the well. It was a long flutter down, and of course it was a bit wet when he landed. But the little red rooster didn't mind. He simply said to himself: 'Come, my empty stomach. Come, my empty stomach and drink up all the water.'

It took a bit of time, but that's just what he did. He drank up all the water, every last drop of it. Up and out of the well he flew, up and away, until he reached the Sultan's window.

'Cockadoodle-doo, Mr Sultana!' he cried. 'Give me back my diamond button.'

The Sultan could not believe his eyes. He could not believe his ears. 'What!' he spluttered. 'You again!' He called his servants. 'Look!' he shrieked. 'Can't you see? That infernal bird is back. I know what I'll do. I know. We'll grab him and throw him into the fire. Let him burn.' So the Sultan's servants rushed at the little red rooster and caught him.

'Aha!' cried the exultant Sultan. 'We've got you

now. You've crowed your very last doodle-doo.'

'I don't think so, Mr Sultana,' said the little red rooster. But the Sultan took him by the neck and threw him on the fire. He wasn't at all frightened of the fire. He knew what to do with fire. He wasn't worried. He simply said to himself: 'Come, my full-up stomach. Come, my full-up stomach, let out all the water and put out all the fire.'

It took a bit of time, but that's just what he did. He gushed out all the water and put out all the fire, every last spark of it. And up he flew again to the Sultan's window.

'Cockadoodle-doo, Mr Sultana,' he cried. 'Give me back my diamond button.'

'What!' spluttered the Sultan. 'You again!'

Now the Sultan was really mad. He was beside himself with fury. He called his servants again. 'Look! That infernal bird is back. I know what I'll do this time. I know. We'll grab him and

throw him into the beehive. Let the bees sting him.' And the Sultan's servants rushed at the little red rooster and caught him.

'Aha!' cried the exultant Sultan. 'We've got you now. You've crowed your very last doodle-doo.'

'I don't think so, Mr Sultana,' said the little red rooster. But the Sultan took him by the neck and threw him into the beehive. The little red rooster wasn't at all frightened by the bees. He knew what to do with bees. He wasn't worried. As the bees buzzed angrily all around him he simply said to himself: 'Come, my empty stomach. Come, my empty stomach and eat up all the bees.'

And that's just what he did. He ate up all the bees, every last one of them.

Back in the palace, the Sultan was rubbing his hands with glee. He thought for sure he had seen the last of the little red rooster. But he hadn't, had he?

He was happily tucking into his lunch of roast peacock, when suddenly he heard this: 'Cocka-doodle-doo, Mr Sultana! Give me back my diamond button.' The little red rooster was back on the window ledge.

'What!' spluttered the Sultan, his mouth full of peacock. 'You again!'

Like a crazed camel, he was, like a vengeful vulture, like a gibbering jackal. He stamped and stormed about the palace, shouting and

screaming at his servants.

'Who will rid me of this infernal bird?' he cried. 'Tell me. Tell me how to do it, or I'll lop off your heads. I will! I will!'

And the servants knew he meant it, too. So naturally they all thought about how they could get rid of the little red rooster. They thought very hard, very hard indeed.

'Hang him by the neck from the pomegranate tree, my lord Sultan,' said one. But the Sultan shook his head.

'Lop off his head, my lord Sultan,' said another.

'It's no good,' wailed the Sultan. 'He'd only run around without it.' And he sat down in deep despair on his cushions.

But then, just as he was sitting down, he heard the cushions sighing and groaning underneath him. He was squashing them flat! 'That's it!' he cried, leaping to his feet. 'I know what I'll do. I know. Grab me that infernal bird. I'll sit on him

and flatten him. I'll squash him. I'll squish him. I'll obsquatulate him!'

From the window ledge the little red rooster heard it all and smiled inside himself.

The Sultan's servants rushed at the little red rooster and caught him.

'Aha!' cried the exultant Sultan. 'We've got you now. You've crowed your very last doodle-doo.'

'I don't think so, Mr Sultana,' said the little red rooster. But the Sultan took the little red rooster by the neck, stuffed him down the back of his pantaloons and then sat down on him hard, very hard indeed.

The little red rooster wasn't at all frightened of being obsquatulated. He knew what to do about that. He wasn't worried. He simply said to himself: 'Come, my full-up stomach. Come, my full-up stomach, let out all the bees and sting the Sultan's bottom.'

And were those bees angry? I should say so.

And did they all sting the great and mighty Sultan's bottom? I should say so. There was plenty of room in those capacious pantaloons for every bee to sting wherever he wanted. And remember, that great and mighty Sultan had a very large, very round bottom, probably the biggest bottom the world had ever seen!

Did the great fat Sultan jump up and down? I should say so. Did he screech and yowl and whimper? I should say so. And did the little red rooster hop out of those great pantaloons and fly off safe and sound? Of course he did.

'Aiee! Ow! Youch! Oosh, oosh, ooh!' cried the Sultan, as he sat with his stinging bottom dunked

in a bath of ice-cold water.

'Cockadoodle-doo, Mr Sultana!' cried the little red rooster. 'Now, will you let me have back my diamond button?'

'All right, all right,' said the Sultan. 'I give in. Anything, anything to get you out of my sight. Take him up to my room and give him his confounded diamond button. It's in my treasure chest.'

So the Sultan's servants took the little red rooster up to the Sultan's bedchamber, and gave him the diamond button from out of the Sultan's treasure chest.

'Now go,' they cried. 'Fly away! Shoo! You've got what you came for. Go, before you get us into any more trouble.'

'I'm going. I'm going,' replied the little red rooster, the diamond button in his beak. But he was in no hurry to go, for something had caught his eye. He could not believe his luck. The

Sultan's treasure chest! The servants had left it open! So he flew away only as far as the window ledge, and he waited there till all the servants had left. Then he flew down and hopped across the room and up on to the treasure chest. Emeralds, rubies, diamonds, pearls, sapphires – the finest jewels in the entire world.

'Ah well. In for a penny, in for a pound,' said the little red rooster to himself. 'Come, my empty stomach. Come, my empty stomach and gobble down all the Sultan's jewels.'

And that's just what he did. He gobbled down all the Sultan's jewels, every last one of them.

Then out he flew, out of the window and out over the palace walls, which was not at all easy, because he was rather heavy by now. He had to waddle all the rest of the way back home, rattling as he went.

As he neared the farm, he happened to meet up with his friends again, the wriggling worms and the singing cicadas and the burrowing beetles. So, of course, he just had to tell them all about his great adventures in the Sultan's palace. He was only halfway through his story when the poor old woman, who had been looking high and low for him, spied him at last. She came scuttling along the farm track.

'Where have you been, Little Red Rooster?' she cried. 'I've been worried sick.'

'Ah, mistress mine,' replied the little red rooster. 'Never in your life will you ever have to worry again. And never will we have to go hungry again, either. Look what I have for you.'

And he said to himself: 'Come, my full-up

stomach. Come, my full-up stomach and give up all your jewels.'

Out they poured on to the ground, all of them, all the Sultan's jewels, until there was a great sparkling pile of them at the poor old woman's feet. Only, she wasn't poor any more, was she?

It took the breath right out of her. She sat down with a bump, still trying to believe her eyes.

'Goodness me!' she cried. 'Goodness me!'

And she *was* good too, goodness itself. Do you know what she did? She gave those jewels to all her poor friends in the countryside round about, just enough for each of them so that no one had too much. She kept for herself all she needed, and no more. But, of course, the little red rooster got to keep his diamond button.

Just you try and take it from him!

The Three Heads in the Well

Retold by Susan Gates

Illustrated by Sue Heap

O nce upon a time, in the east of this land, ruled the King of Colchester. Everything in his life seemed as sweet as honey. All his enemies had been well and truly conquered. His kingdom was peaceful; his subjects were loyal. He himself was brave and strong. But, in the middle of his happiness, disaster struck. His Queen died and he was left alone to care for their only daughter – a princess famed far and wide for her smiling face and

her kind and generous nature.

The King of Colchester looked about him for a new wife. He found a rich widow. Her riches were the only thing to recommend her, for she was a sour-faced, scowling woman, boiling with envy and spite. This widow too, had an only daughter. And the daughter was like the mother. Both were as mean-spirited as the King's daughter was generous. As sly and scheming as the King's daughter was honest and open-hearted.

Servants gossiped in the castle kitchens. They whispered in corridors. 'His Majesty is making a serious mistake,' they said. 'He'll live to regret it.' Some high-ranking nobles even dared to warn him to his face. But the King waved them all angrily away. He would listen to no one. He married the wealthy widow out of greed for her riches. And that was his only reason. For he didn't love her – not one jot.

No sooner were they in the castle than the King's new wife and her daughter got busy. They began to make trouble and cause upsets and bad feeling. They were very good at it. Rumours flew everywhere, like flocks of crows. They were particularly jealous of the young Princess because everyone loved her.

'We must get rid of her!' hissed mother to daughter.

With dark plots, sly schemes and whispering campaigns, they poisoned the King's mind against his own daughter. The Princess saw that, day by day, her father's heart grew colder towards her. But she, poor innocent girl, was useless at plotting. She was powerless

to stop the wicked pair.

Soon, the court became an unfriendly place. Cold looks were cast in her direction. Her own father did not have a single kind thing to say about her. Sick at heart, she decided to leave to seek her fortune in the wide world. The King's new wife and step-daughter agreed that this was an excellent idea.

The Princess met her father the King as he strolled in his rose garden, sniffing the roses. She said, her eyes brimming with tears, 'Father, may I have your consent to go and seek my fortune?' He didn't say one warm word to persuade her to stay. He gave his consent, then waved her coldly away.

And so the Princess was driven away from her home. Even though she'd got her wish, the step-mother was mean-minded to the last. She gave the Princess only four things to take on her journey – a canvas bag, some brown bread, some mousetrap cheese and a bottle of beer. A swine-herd's daughter would have been treated more generously than this! But, even though these were the stingiest gifts imaginable, the Princess thanked her step-mother and set out on her journey.

She walked through valleys and meadows and dark, tangled woods. At last, when she was almost fainting from weariness and misery she saw an old man. He was perched on a rock at the mouth of a cave.

'Good morrow, fair maiden,' he greeted her. 'And where are you off to this fine day?'

'I'm going to seek my fortune, aged father,' she answered him.

'And what have you got in that canvas bag?'

'Bread and cheese,' said the Princess, 'and a bottle of beer. Are you hungry or thirsty? You are welcome to share it.'

So the old man ate and drank his fill. Afterwards, he thanked her with all his heart and gave her some good words of advice. 'Soon,' he said, 'you will come to a thick, thorny hedge. It will seem impassable. But take this wand, strike the hedge three times and say, "Pray hedge, let me through!" The hedge will part to let you through. A little further on you will come to a well. Sit down at the edge of it and three Golden Heads will appear to you. When they speak, you must be sure to do what they tell you.'

The Princess promised to follow the old man's instructions. She said, 'Farewell,' and set out once again on her journey.

Soon she came to the hedge. It was thick and high. It bristled with cruel spiky thorns. It

seemed impossible to get through. But the Princess remembered the old man's words. She took the wand, struck the hedge three times and, with each blow, said, 'Pray hedge, let me through.'

Instantly, the cruel thorns drew in, like a cat's claws. The hedge parted to make her a doorway. She was able to pass through safely without even a tiny rip in her dress.

A little further on the Princess came to a well. She sat down on the edge of it, as the old man had told her. To tell the truth, she was happy to rest her weary bones. She had been walking, poor girl, since daybreak. And Princesses have very tender feet!

But no sooner had she sat down, than up, from the dark depths of the well, popped a Golden Head. In a voice clear and sweet as the well water, it sang:

> *'Wash me, comb me,*
> *And lay me down softly,*
> *And lay me on a bank to dry,*
> *That I may look pretty,*
> *When someone passes by.'*

The Princess spread her skirts and lifted the Golden Head into her lap. Taking a silver comb, she gently combed its hair, humming as she did so. Then she set the Head on a primrose bank beside her to dry.

Then a second Golden Head rose up and a third! Both sang the same request:

'Wash me, comb me,
And lay me down softly,
And lay me on a bank to dry,
That I may look pretty,
When someone passes by.'

And the Princess did them the same kind service. She took each in her lap and combed their golden locks with the silver comb until they were smooth and free of tangles. Then she opened her canvas bag and ate her dinner, while the three Golden Heads lay beside her, drying their hair in the sunshine.

As they snuggled side by side among the primroses, the Heads had a secret conversation. They whispered into each other's ears: 'How shall we repay this maid, who has used us so kindly?'

The first Head said, 'I will make her even more beautiful, so she may charm any Prince she pleases.'

The second said, 'I will perfume her body and breath, so she smells sweeter than the sweetest flowers.'

The third said, 'I will give her the good fortune to marry the most powerful King in the land.'

When the Princess had finished her bread and cheese, the three Heads said, 'Pray, place us back in the water.' She did so. They sank to the bottom of the well in a swirl of bubbles.

The Princess went on her way. She had not gone far before she heard a hunting horn, 'Ta ra! Ta ra!' She saw a young King out riding in the park with his nobles. They were a merry crowd. Their rich clothes glowed with beautiful colours. She

hurried to hide behind an oak tree, ashamed of her rags. For, I forgot to say, her spiteful step-mother had allowed her to leave the castle in only the meanest, drabbest clothes. Worse than a kitchen maid would wear!

But it was too late, the young King had spotted her. He came towards her. He saw her beautiful face, smelled her fragrant, flowery breath and, instantly, he fell head-over-heels in love. He soon melted her heart, with compliments and kisses. Joyfully, they went back to his palace where his court ladies dressed her from top to toe in splendid, rich clothes.

As soon as she told him that she was the King of Colchester's daughter, he cried, 'Make ready my royal chariot. We must pay your father a visit!'

The King of Colchester was amazed when the royal chariot, all crusted with gold and jewels, came dashing up to his castle gates. He was even more astonished when he learned that his own

daughter was inside it. And that the mightiest King in the land wanted her to be his Queen. There was much making-up and hugging and rejoicing. The marriage feast lasted for days and days! Eventually the young King and his new Queen went back to their own kingdom. The royal chariot was piled high with the treasures the King of Colchester had given his daughter as her dowry.

So everyone was happy at the Princess's good fortune. Except, of course, for the step-mother and her sour-faced daughter. They didn't dance one single step at the wedding. They didn't let one single sugared almond or sip of sweet wine pass their lips. Their mouths looked as if they'd been

sucking on lemons. Their jealousy and spite carried on swelling and swelling inside them. Until they almost burst at the seams with envy! Especially as the Princess was now the highest Queen in the land and vastly more important and wealthy than either of them.

Finally the daughter said to her mother, 'Mother, I have made up my mind! Put out my finest clothes. Pack me up some delicious food, such as fine white bread and sugar plums and lots of other sweetmeats. Oh, and don't forget a large bottle of your best Malaga Sack as I am bound to get thirsty on my journey.'

'What journey are you talking about, daughter?' enquired the mother.

'I have made up my mind to follow the same road as my step-sister,' declared the daughter. 'I am going to seek my fortune. And I know I shall find it for I'm sure I deserve it more than she!'

In her richest clothes and almost bent double under the weight of all her provisions, the sister set out on her journey.

Soon, puffing and panting, she reached the cave where the old man sat on a rock.

'Young woman,' he said, 'you carry a heavy burden. What do you have in that large bag you're carrying?'

'Mind your own business!' replied the sister, nastily. 'I have good food in here but it's nothing for you to be troubled with.'

'From the look of that bag you have more than enough for one. You have enough for a whole army! I am very old; I barely eat more than a sparrow. So won't you spare me a bite of food or a drop of drink?'

'Not unless it chokes you!' replied the sister, rudely. 'Not a drop or a bite or even a sniff of this good food will you get from me, old man!'

The old man's face grew grim. He frowned.

'Then evil fortune attend you!' he said, as she went on her way.

Soon, the thorny hedge blocked her path. She thought, How can I pass through there?

Then she imagined she spied a gap. She plunged into the hedge. But its branches closed round her like a thousand spiky arms. She struggled and fought to escape, cursing the hedge with every spare breath. At last, the hedge let her through. But by now, she was in a sorry state. All her fine clothes were in tatters and blood trickled down where the thorns had pricked her.

She looked round for water to wash in. Then she saw the well. She sat down at its edge and washed and began to unpack all her food,

meaning to enjoy a good feast.

A Golden Head plopped up to the top of the well.

> '*Wash me, comb me,*' it sang,
> '*And lay me down softly,*
> *And lay me on a bank to dry,*
> *That I may look pretty,*
> *When someone passes by.*'

The sister jumped up, furious that her dinner had been interrupted.

'Hang you! Take that for your washing!' she cried and, whack! she hit the Golden Head a dreadful blow with her bottle of Malaga Sack.

The second and third Heads came up but she treated them no better than the first. Whack, whack! She swiped at them with her bottle of Malaga Sack, then sat down to tuck into her sugar plums.

So, while the sister ate, the three Heads bobbed about like corks in the water, whispering amongst themselves. They said, 'How shall we repay this maid, who has used us so cruelly?'

The first said, 'Let her have a mangy face, all covered in spots and boils.'

The second said, 'Let her breath become even more stinking, so that people run away when she approaches.'

The third said, 'Let her find a husband. Let him not be a prince but only a poor and humble country cobbler.'

The sister hardly noticed when the Golden Heads sank back into the well. She finished her dinner and went on her way.

She came to a town. It was bustling with people because it was market day. As she turned into the market square a few people caught a whiff of her breath.

They looked about them. 'Phew! What is that terrible pong?' they asked each other, holding their noses. It smelled worse than a million muck heaps.

Then, as she walked nearer, everyone smelled it. It filled the market square like a stinking cloud. People rushed to escape. They were in such a panic they uptipped the stalls and trampled each other underfoot! Soon the market square was completely empty – except for one person. The sister was relieved to see him, even though he

was only a poor country cobbler.

Now, not long before, this same cobbler had mended the sandals of an old hermit. The hermit had no money to pay him. So instead he gave the cobbler a box of ointment for clearing up mangy faces and a bottle of spirits for making foul breath sweet again. This cobbler felt sorry for the unfortunate sister afflicted with stinks and spots. Holding his nose, he approached her. He could see that she was a fine lady, even though her clothes were in tatters. 'Who are you?' he asked her.

'I am,' said she, 'the King of Colchester's step-daughter.'

'Well, King of Colchester's step-daughter,' said the poor cobbler, 'I've got an offer to make to you. These are my terms. If I cure your stinking breath and clear up your spotty complexion, will you reward me by taking me as your husband?'

'Yes, friend,' replied the sister, gratefully. 'I will do it. With all my heart.'

So, every day, the sister gargled with the spirits and smeared the ointment all over her face and in a few weeks she was cured. She kept her word and married the poor cobbler. Then they set off for the court at Colchester to tell her mother the news.

The Queen was not overjoyed to see her daughter. In fact, when she found out that she had married a humble cobbler, she fell into a shrieking fury. Her frightful screams echoed through the castle. Rats rushed out of drains. Pigeons plummeted off ramparts. Servants

quaked in corners. Even the King trembled in his boots. The Queen's fury became a raging madness and she topped it all off by hanging herself, out of spite.

The King gave her a splendid funeral. But, since he was so pleased to get rid of her, you may be sure he cried only crocodile tears. After the funeral, he gave the cobbler one hundred pounds, on condition that he and his lady quit the court for ever.

'Gladly!' cried the cobbler, who couldn't believe his luck.

He took his wife and his hundred pounds and set up his business far away from the court, in a remote part of the kingdom. And there they lived, not unhappily, for many years – the cobbler mending shoes and his wife spinning thread.

And so ends the tale, 'The Three Heads in the Well.'

The Little Mermaid

Hans Christian Andersen

Retold by Linda Newbery

Illustrated by Bee Willey

Imagine!

Far, far out to sea, the water is bluer than blue, and clearer than the clearest crystal glass. Imagine you can swim there – down, down to the deepest depths, where no human has ever been. Here is a row of little gardens – each one decorated with shells, and planted with seaweed that waves in the current like hair.

Here, by a marble statue, sits a little mermaid. In her garden, where fish dart in and out like

swallows and the water thrums like the song of a harp, the little mermaid is unhappy. She neither sees the fish nor hears the lull of the water-song.

'If only I were fifteen!' she sighs.

She has five older sisters, this mermaid. All are princesses – daughters of the mer-king, whose splendid palace is crusted all over with coral, amber and pearls. The mermaid princesses have lost their mother, but otherwise have everything they could possibly want. All except the young-est, the little mermaid.

She longs to see the world of humans above the water.

For this, a mermaid must wait for her fifteenth birthday. Then she may swim to the surface and sit on a rock, or lie on a sandbank – to see, and to listen. All her sisters have passed fifteen now; each has made her journey, has seen cities and palaces and carriages, and humans walking about on their two legs; and each has decided that the underwater world is best, and is happy to stay there.

But the youngest mermaid looks at her statue, and dreams. It is a statue of a handsome young man. She found it on the sea-bed, lost from a shipwreck, and has planted her garden round it. Sometimes she sings to it, for she has the most beautiful voice. She gazes at its marble face, and fancies that in the human world above, there will be a living face to match it.

At last, the day of her birthday!

'Goodbye!' she called to her sisters and her

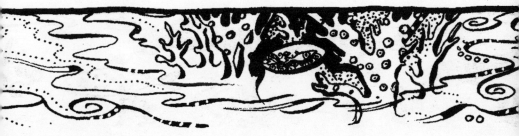

grandmother, and she rose through the water on her first journey to the world of humans. Cautiously she peeped above the surface, not knowing what she would see. It was a calm, still evening, with the sky lit rose-pink. Seeing a splendid three-masted ship, she swam closer. There was barely a breath of wind and the ship was almost still. The little mermaid looked through the cabin windows and saw people and lanterns and tables decked with food.

Her eyes went straight to a beautiful prince, who reminded her of her statue. It seemed to be his birthday; the party was in his honour.

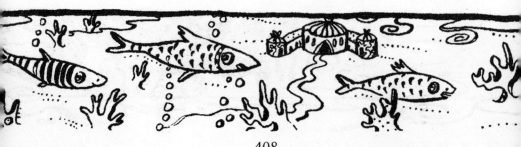

'His birthday, and mine!' she thought.

At midnight, the lanterns were dimmed and the guests went to bed. The waves swelled, rolling the ship to and fro. The wind rushed in, filling the sails; the sky was heavy with clouds. The mermaid, who understood the sea and its weather, knew there would be a fearful storm. To her, a wild sea was a playground – she dashed and dived through surging waves, and rode high on their crests.

But it was no game for the ship. The sailors heaved on ropes and pulled in sails, but the ship was as frail as a paper boat on a pond. The wind struck again and again, and water rushed over the deck. The timbers creaked and groaned; and then one mighty blast snapped the main mast and sent the whole ship keeling over.

Now the little mermaid had to look after her own safety, dodging the cracked timbers and the splinters of wreckage. She saw the young prince

flung into the water, swimming, and sinking – at first she was delighted, for now he would come to live underwater. But then she remembered that human beings cannot survive in water – only if the prince were dead could he visit her father's palace.

No! He mustn't die!

She dived deep, and caught him as he sank, pulled down by the current. His eyes were closed, his limbs already numb. She swam hard, pushing up to the surface with all the muscular strength of her tail. All through the night, the little mermaid held him, supporting him till her arms and tail ached with weariness.

Dawn came, and the first light lit the prince's face. She kissed him and prayed that he would live. She sang to him, just as she sang to her statue. She swam, not knowing where to take him.

At last she saw land – snow-clad mountains, green forests and a holy temple. She carried her prince to the bay, and laid him to rest on the sand. Soon, people came from the temple. A dark-haired girl called out and ran to the shore, and suddenly there was a great commotion – one person tipped the prince face-down, another slapped his cheeks, the young girl rubbed his hands. The mermaid, hiding behind rocks, watched and watched – and at last he coughed and spluttered, and sat up. He was alive! There were exclamations of joy and relief. The prince, gaining strength, smiled at the young girl who held his hand, and spoke to the people around him; they wrapped him in a cloak, and led him away.

The little mermaid was glad that he was alive –
but sad that he had smiled at all those people but
never once at her, for he did not know who his
real rescuer was.

She returned to the mer-king's palace, silent
and thoughtful.

'Well?' her sisters asked her. 'Where did you
go? What did you see? What did you do?'

But the little mermaid went to sit in her garden
by herself. Mermaids cannot shed tears, or she
would have wept.

Many a time, in the following days, she swam
to the shore by the temple. She saw people come
and go, heard their chatter, but never once did

she see her handsome prince.

At last she could bear it no longer. She whispered her secret to one of her sisters.

'I know who you mean! I can show you where his palace is!' said the sister. The magnificent palace faced the seashore. It was built of glistening stone, with great flights of marble steps. There were statues, fountains, domes. There was a garden, whose flowers and greenery looked to the little mermaid far superior to the straggles of weed in her own garden.

Day by day she grew fascinated by the world of humans. She would rise from the water and gaze at the palace, longing for a glimpse of her love. Growing braver, she swam up the river inlet, next to the marble terrace. Often she saw him – strolling in the garden, or sailing, or talking to friends.

One evening, she swam back and sought out her wise grandmother.

'If humans don't drown,' she asked, 'do they live for ever? Or do they die as we do, after three hundred years?'

'Oh yes, they die,' said the grandmother, 'and their lives are much shorter than ours. But when we die, we turn into foam on the sea, and that's the end of us. Humans have immortal souls – their souls live for ever, among the stars, in places we can only dream of!'

'Why can't we have immortal souls?' asked the little mermaid. 'I'd give anything to be human! I'd give up some of my three hundred years if I could live for ever in that place in the stars!'

'Don't talk like that, silly girl!' the grand-mother chided. 'We're much better off down here.' And she called an angel fish to her, and fed it from her hand.

'Is there no way I can get an immortal soul?' persisted the little mermaid.

'There's only one way,' said the grandmother.

'If you can get a human man to love you, to wish more than anything to marry you, to be bound to you for all eternity – then he'll give you an immortal soul, while keeping his own.' Then she laughed, and pointed to their tails. 'But how can that happen? Our tails, our greatest beauty, are thought by humans to be monstrous. For them to find you pretty, you need two of those stumpy things they call legs.'

'Oh,' said the mermaid, looking down at her green scaly tail.

'Cheer up!' said the grandmother. 'There's a ball tonight, and you're to sing. We know how to enjoy ourselves, in our three hundred years.'

That evening the princess sang and everyone admired her voice, which was far more beautiful than the voice of any human. The palace was flooded with light, and all kinds of fish, great and small, colourful as fragments from a kaleidoscope, came to watch the festivities.

Everyone danced and laughed and ate – everyone but the little mermaid, who only wanted to dream of her prince in the world above. She left the palace to sit alone in her garden.

I love him, yet he doesn't know I exist, she thought. I'd give anything to be with him!

She knew of only one person who might help her – the sea-witch, of whom everyone was afraid. But the little mermaid was ready to risk anything to win the love of her prince.

While it was still dark, the little mermaid ventured across deserts of sand and through roaring whirlpools. Beyond, the sea-witch lived in a

cave in the midst of a weird forest. The trees and bushes were half-human, half-animal – they stretched and leered at the little mermaid. She hesitated, afraid to pass through. Some clasped bones of drowned fishermen in their tentacles; others reached out their slimy arms to grab her. She almost lost heart and turned back; then she thought of her prince, closed her eyes and darted, slick as quicksilver, past the monstrous trees to the cave beyond.

There sat the sea-witch, with water-snakes crawling all over her and in and out of her hair.

'I know why you've come!' she said straight away. 'And you shall have it, for it will lead you into trouble. You want to exchange your fish's tail for two ugly stumps, like humans have. You want that prince to fall in love with you, and give you an immortal soul. Yes?'

'Yes,' confessed the mermaid.

The sea-witch laughed so loudly that all the

snakes fell out of her hair and wriggled about on the slimy sea-bed.

'I'll make you a potion,' she said, 'and you must swim to a sand-bank near this prince's palace, then drink it up. Your tail will shrivel up and divide into two stumps, that men call legs, and then you'll be able to walk on land. But it will hurt! It will feel like a sharp sword slicing through you. And every step you take will feel like walking on knives. Are you stupid enough to do all that, for this man you hardly know?'

'Yes,' said the mermaid, trembling.

The witch laughed nastily. 'Yes, I thought so. Remember, you'll never be a mermaid again – you'll never see your sisters, or your grandmother, or your father's palace. And if the prince doesn't love you more than anyone else, you won't get an immortal soul! If he marries someone else, your heart will break, and the very next morning you'll turn into foam of the sea. Still want to do it?'

'Yes,' said the mermaid, shivering.

'Then,' said the witch, 'you must pay me. Your voice is more beautiful than anyone's – I'm having that, for my wages. You're not going to charm him that way!'

'But with no voice,' said the little mermaid, 'what have I left?'

'Your lovely face,' sneered the witch. 'Your beautiful shape. Your speaking eyes. That's enough, isn't it, to bewitch a mere man? Oh, having second thoughts, are you? Not such a good idea, now?'

'I'll do it!' said the little mermaid, on a surge of defiance.

The witch laughed and scoured her cauldron with a handful of snakes. Then she slit her little finger and let the black blood drip into the pot. She threw in more ingredients – sea-slugs, rotting weed, toad-slime. Foul-smelling steam rose from the cauldron and took the shape of grinning faces. At last the potion was brewed and the liquid turned clear.

'All done!' said the witch, sniffing it. She poured some into a glass vial. 'Now, my price.'

And she pointed a knobbly finger at the little mermaid's mouth. At once, the mermaid's tongue burned and shrivelled to nothing. She tried to speak, but could not make a sound.

'Now go away,' said the witch, settling down for a rest with her snakes and toads.

The little mermaid swam quickly back to her father's palace, clutching the vial. The palace was still in darkness and everyone still asleep. The little mermaid dared not go in; instead, she swam

through all her sisters' gardens, plucking one flower from each. Mermaids cannot shed tears, or she would have wept.

The sun had not yet risen when she reached the shore facing the prince's palace. She swam to the marble steps, and there she drank the potion. It burned and stung her poor shrivelled tongue and her throat; and at once she felt the sharpest, most unbearable pain slicing through her. She gave a soundless scream and fainted.

She woke to daylight and a fresh stab of pain; and then she saw that her prince had come! His coal-black eyes were looking at her, tender and

anxious. She looked down and saw that she had a pair of slender legs instead of her tail; but she was naked, so she wrapped her long hair around her body.

'Who are you? Where have you come from?' the prince asked, kneeling.

She could not tell him; she looked at him yearningly. He took her hand and helped her up. She took her first steps on human feet – and each step, just as the sea-witch had said, was like treading on sharp knives. But she would not let the pain show in her face; she clutched her hair around her and smiled gratefully.

Everyone in the palace marvelled at her beauty. She was given fine clothes, and good things to eat; but she was dumb, and could not thank them.

There were parties, and the little mermaid wished so desperately that she could sing to her prince, to tell him of her love. She could only applaud other singers whose voices sounded cracked and strained, compared to the memory of her own water-music.

Instead, she danced for him. She was the most graceful dancer in the palace, even though with each twirling step, each pirouette, she felt the stab of a hundred razor-sharp daggers. When the dancing was over, and everyone in bed, she went outside to paddle in the sea, letting the water cool her burning feet. And she fancied that in the shimmer of moonlight on water she saw her mermaid sisters, raising their heads to call to her and stretching out their arms.

She became the prince's favourite companion, and spent every day and evening with him. He loved her; but not as she wanted to be loved.

'There's only one girl I'll ever marry,' he told her as they sat together one evening. 'You remind me of her – the girl who rescued me!'

The little mermaid gazed at him, her eyes imploring. Had he opened his eyes after all, while he was lifeless in the water – had he seen her?

'But I'll never win her love,' the prince said sadly. 'She belongs to the holy temple. She lives a life of prayer and contemplation. What use has she for husband, marriage or home? Yet I owe her my life! I would have drowned had

she not pulled me from the sea!'

No! No! The little mermaid tried to tell him. *I* was the one who saved you, who pulled you from the deeps and used all my strength to support you!

'I shall never forget that beautiful face!' said the prince, half to himself; then he turned to the mermaid. 'You understand, don't you? There is a sadness about you. You understand what it is to long for something with your heart and soul and to be denied it?'

Oh yes, she understood!

'And now I'm to visit the king of the next country,' the prince grumbled. 'They expect me to marry his daughter, but I shan't! I'll marry no one but my girl of the temple. You'll come with me, won't you my dearest friend, to while away the tedium?'

The prince's new ship set sail, and the prince stood on deck with the little mermaid, telling her

of the wonders of the deep: the strange creatures, the dark caverns, the marvels that even divers had not seen. She smiled to hear him talk, for she knew much better than he! And she longed for the visit to be over, and to have her beloved prince to herself again, for she knew he had no interest in the foreign king's daughter.

When the prince's ship docked in the harbour of the magnificent city, there were parties, and processions, and parades, and the prince was always the guest of honour – but of the king's daughter there was no sign.

'She will be here soon,' the little mermaid heard

one of the court attendants say, 'when she comes back from her studies at the holy temple. And then there will be a wedding, for this prince cannot help but fall in love with her. What a fine pair they will make! For she is his match in beauty, grace and wealth.'

At the words 'holy temple', the little mermaid shivered, for she knew now who the king's daughter was, and that the prince loved her already. The young girl came home two days later and shyly greeted her future husband. When the little mermaid saw the lovely face, the long dark hair and shining eyes, she felt a cold tremor pass through her. She would never win the prince's love now, for he was overjoyed to find himself paired with his true love, the girl from the holy temple, the girl he believed had saved him.

'You're happy for me, aren't you, my dear friend?' the prince asked the little mermaid, the

night before the wedding. 'I am happier than I ever dreamed! But you will always be my friend – and hers! For she must love you as well as I do.'

The wedding was a splendid occasion. Bells pealed and heralds trumpeted, and the church was decked with flowers. The bride and groom, gorgeously dressed, held hands and were blessed by the bishop, and proclaimed husband and wife. The little mermaid, dressed in silk and gold, held the bride's train. But she heard and saw little of the ceremony – she could think only of her coming death, and of all that she had gained, and lost.

The wedding party that night was held on board the prince's ship. When the dancing began, the little mermaid remembered the first night she had danced for her prince. She would dance again, for the very last time! And she threw herself into the music, skimming, twirling, whirling, and everyone stopped dancing to cheer her. Each step sent pain searing through her feet, yet she hardly noticed, for the pain in her heart was much sharper.

At last the prince and his bride went to their royal bed and the little mermaid stood alone on the deck, gazing out to sea. She would die with the first rays of dawn light. She would never see her beloved prince again, nor have an immortal soul.

Out on the bobbing waves, she saw the glimmer of pale faces, and arms stretched towards her. Her sisters! But she stared – how strange they looked! Their long hair had

gone, sheared to stubble!

'Sister!' they called. 'We've given our hair to the sea-witch, to make her help us! Do what we tell you!' The mermaid saw the flash of moonlight on steel. 'Take this knife! Before the sun rises, you must plunge it into the prince's heart! When his blood sprinkles your feet, they'll disappear and turn back into your mermaid's tail, and you'll be able to come home with us and live out your three hundred years! But hurry! Can't you see how the sky is lightening?'

The little mermaid reached down for the knife and her sisters sank beneath the water.

With heavy heart, she crept into the prince's bedroom. There he slept, with his lovely bride cradled close; the little mermaid kissed him and then he murmured the name of his bride, his beloved. He had no thought for anyone but her!

The little mermaid raised the knife – how heavy it was, and how sharp! – and held it poised. She thought of all the cutting pain she had endured for his sake.

Then, making her choice, she lowered it. She ran to the deck, and with all her strength hurled the dagger into the waves. For a second it hung in the air, catching the first rosy dawn light.

Her eyes already dimming, she threw herself overboard and her body dissolved into foam of the sea.

Now the sun rose, and its kindly beams warmed the foam, so that the little mermaid did not feel the chill of death. Instead, she saw the

sun, and the air above, filled with wispy shapes and silvery voices.

'Where am I going?' she asked.

A voice replied, 'You are with the Daughters of the Air! You, poor little mermaid, had no immortal soul, but you have yearned for something with your whole heart, and now you are rewarded for your good deeds! Come with us!'

And the little mermaid saw that she had a new shape, a wispy, transparent shape like theirs, risen out of the foam. Together they floated, light as bubbles, laughing.

She gazed down at the ship, and thought of her prince lying there asleep, his arms entwined with his bride's. She felt sad for him; he would never know where she had gone, or what she had done for him.

'Come sister! Fly higher!' urged the silvery voice. 'For our spirit world is more beautiful

432

than you can ever imagine.'

The little mermaid looked up into the golden, streaming light, and at her new sisters, the Daughters of the Air. Then she looked down towards her prince for the last time. She must leave him now.

'Goodbye,' she whispered; and for the first time she shed tears.

About the Authors

Malorie Blackman's books have won several awards, including the Children's Book Award for *Noughts and Crosses*. She has also won the W. H. Smith Mind-Boggling Books Award and the Young Telegraph/Gimme 5 Award, as well as being shortlisted for the Carnegie Medal. *Pig-Heart Boy* was adapted into a BAFTA-award-winning TV serial. In 2008 Malorie was honoured with an OBE for her services to Children's Literature.

Henrietta Branford was born in India in 1946 but grew up in a remote part of the New Forest. Her first novel, *Royal Blunder*, was published in 1990. After that she wrote many different sorts of books, from picture books to teenage novels, including *Dimanche Diller* (Smarties Prize and the Prix Tam-Tam) and *Fire, Bed and Bone* (Guardian Children's Fiction Prize). After her death in 1997 a prize was established to commemorate her and her editor Wendy Boase – the Branford Boase Award for a first novel.

Gillian Cross was born in 1945. Although she is now a full-time writer, she has had a number of informal jobs, including being an assistant to a

Member of Parliament. Her books include *Wolf* (Carnegie Medal 1990), *The Great Elephant Chase* (Whitbread Children's Book Award, Smarties Prize, 1992) and the titles in the 'Demon Headmaster' sequence, which was also made into a TV series.

Berlie Doherty began writing for children in 1982, after teaching and working in radio. She has written more than thirty-five books for children, as well as for the theatre, radio and television. She has won the Carnegie Medal twice: in 1986 for *Granny Was a Buffer Girl* and in 1991 for *Dear Nobody*. She has also won the Writer's Guild Children's Fiction Award for *Daughter of the Sea*. Her work is published all over the world, and many of her books have been televised.

Anne Fine has been an acknowledged top author in the children's book world since her first book, *The Summer-House Loon*, was published in 1978, and has now written more than fifty books and won virtually every major award, including the Carnegie Medal (more than once), the Whitbread Children's Book Award, the Guardian Children's Fiction Prize, the Smarties Prize and others. Anne Fine was the Children's Laureate from 2001–2003. Her best-known books include *Madame Doubtfire* (which was made into the film *Mrs Doubtfire*), *Goggle-Eyes* and *Flour Babies*.

Alan Garner OBE (born in Congleton, Cheshire, in 1934) spent his childhood in Alderley Edge, Cheshire. Many of his works, including *The Weirdstone of Brisingamen* and its sequel *The Moon of Gomrath*, are drawn from local legends. *The Owl Service* won both the Guardian Children's Fiction Prize and the Carnegie Medal in 1968. *The Stone Book* (which received the Phoenix Award in 1996) is poetic in style and inspiration. His collection of essays and public talks, *The Voice That Thunders*, contains autobiographical material as well as critical reflection upon folklore and language, literature and education, the nature of myth and time.

Susan Gates was born in Grimsby, England. Before she became a full-time writer she lived and worked in Malawi, Africa, then taught in schools in Coventry and County Durham in England. She has written more than 100 books for children, many of which have won prizes. She has been overall winner of the Sheffield Children's Book Award twice, commended for the Carnegie Medal, and Highly Commended for the Nasen Special Educational Needs Award.

Adèle Geras was born in Jerusalem and travelled widely as a child. She started writing over thirty years ago and has published more than eighty books for children and young adults. *Ithaka* was shortlisted for the Guardian Children's Fiction Prize and the Whitbread Children's Book Award. She lives in Cambridge with her husband, and has two grown-up daughters and two grandchildren.

Tony Mitton is an award-winning poet, whose delightful verse has proved enormously success-ful with both adults and children, particularly in picture books. He has written for reading schemes and flip-the-flap books, but is best-known for such series as *Rap Rhymes*, *Amazing Machines* and *Amazing Animals* as well as his own poetry books. He lives in Cambridge with his wife and two children.

Michael Morpurgo is one of today's most popular and critically acclaimed children's writers, author of *War Horse* (made into an enor-mously successful stage play) and *The Wreck of The Zanzibar* amongst many other titles. He has won a multitude of prizes, including the Whitbread Children's Book Award, the Smarties Prize and the Writer's Guild Award. Michael Morpurgo's work is noted for its magical use of storytelling, for characters' relationships with nature, and for vivid settings.

Linda Newbery is the author of over twenty-five books for children and young adults, including

At the Firefly Gate (nominated for the Carnegie Medal), *Catcall* (Silver Medal, Nestlé Children's Book Prize), *Set in Stone* (Costa Children's Book Prize), *Sisterland* (shortlisted for the Carnegie Medal) and *The Shell House* (shortlisted for the Carnegie Medal and the Guardian Children's Fiction Prize). She lives in an Oxfordshire village with her husband.

Philip Pullman is one of the most highly acclaimed children's authors. He has been on the shortlist of just about every major children's book award in the last few years, and has won the Smarties Prize for *The Firework-Maker's Daughter* and the Carnegie Medal for *Northern Lights*. He was the first children's author ever to win the overall Whitbread Book Award (for his novel *The Amber Spyglass*). A film of *Northern Lights* (titled *The Golden Compass*) was made in 2008 by New Line Cinema. He lives in Oxford.

Jacqueline Wilson is one of the world's most popular authors for younger readers. She served as Children's Laureate from 2005–7. *The Illustrated Mum* was chosen as the British Children's Book of the Year in 1999 and was winner of the Guardian Children's Fiction Prize in 2000. She has won the Smarties Prize and the Children's Book Award for *Double Act*, which was also highly commended for the Carnegie Medal. In 2002 she was given an OBE for services to literacy in schools, and in 2008 was appointed a Dame.

Kit Wright was born in 1944 and is the author of more than twenty-five books, for both adults and children. His books of poetry include *The Bear Looked Over the Mountain* (1977), which won the Geoffrey Faber Memorial Prize and the Alice Hunt Bartlett Award, and *Short Afternoons* (1989), which won the Hawthornden Prize and was joint winner of the Heinemann Award. His poetry is collected in *Hoping It Might Be So: Poems 1974–2000* (2000).

Acknowledgements and Publication Details

The Six Swan Brothers first published by Scholastic in 1998. Text copyright © Adèle Geras, 1998. Illustrations copyright © Ian Beck, 1998.

The Twelve Dancing Princesses first published by Scholastic in 1998. Text copyright © Anne Fine, 1998. Illustrations copyright © Debi Gliori, 1998.

Hansel and Gretel first published by Scholastic in 1998. Text copyright © Henrietta Branford, 1998. Illustrations copyright © Lesley Harker, 1998.

Rapunzel first published by Scholastic in 1998. Text copyright © Jacqueline Wilson, 1998. Illustrations copyright © Nick Sharratt, 1998.

Aesop's Fables first published by Scholastic in 1998. Text copyright © Malorie Oneta Blackman, 1998. Illustrations copyright © Patrice Aggs, 1998.

Mossycoat first published by Scholastic in 1998. Text copyright © Philip Pullman, 1998. Illustrations copyright © Peter Bailey, 1998.

The Seal Hunter first published by Scholastic in 1998. Text copyright © Tony Mitton, 1998. Illustrations copyright © Nick Maland, 1998.

Grey Wolf, Prince Jack and the Firebird first published by Scholastic in 1998. Text copyright © Alan Garner, 1998. Illustrations copyright © James Mayhew, 1998.

The Snow Queen first published by Scholastic in 1998. Text copyright © Berlie Doherty, 1998. Illustrations copyright © Siân Bailey, 1998.

The Goose Girl first published by Scholastic in 1998. Text copyright © Gillian Cross, 1998. Illustrations copyright © Peter Bailey, 2011.

Rumpelstiltskin first published by Scholastic in 1998. Text copyright © Kit Wright, 1998. Illustrations copyright © Ted Dewan, 1998.

Cockadoodle-doo, Mr Sultana! first published by Scholastic in 1998. Text copyright © Michael Morpurgo, 1998. Illustrations copyright © Michael Foreman, 1998.

The Three Heads in the Well first published by Scholastic in 1998. Text copyright © Susan Gates, 1998. Illustrations copyright © Sue Heap, 1998.

The Little Mermaid first published by Scholastic in 2001. Text copyright © Linda Newbery, 2001. Illustrations copyright © Bee Willey, 2001.